NIGHTWORK

NIGHTWORK

STORIES

CHRISTINE SCHUTT

ALFRED A. KNOPF   NEW YORK 1996

"The Summer After Barbara Claffey," "You Drive," "Good Night,
Sweetheart," "What Have You Been Doing?" "An Unseen Hand Passed over
Their Bodies," "Daywork," "Teachers," "See If You Can Lift Me," "The
Enchantment," "Because I Could Not Stop for Death," and "Giovanni
and Giovanna" were first published in *The Quarterly*. "Religion" was published
in *StoryQuarterly*. "His Chorus" was published in *The Alaska Quarterly*, and
"Metropolis" was published in *The Mississippi Review*. "To Have and to Hold"
originally appeared in the anthology *The Unmade Bed*, published by
HarperCollins Publishers.

Library of Congress Cataloging-in-Publication Data
Schutt, Christine.
Nightwork : stories / by Christine Schutt.—1st ed.
    p. cm.
ISBN 0-679-40451-1
1. Manners and customs—Fiction. I. Title.
PS3569.C55555N54 1996
813'.54—dc20 95-32033 CIP

Manufactured in the United States of America
First Edition

TO NICK AND WILL

CONTENTS

CONTENTS

NIGHTWORK

YOU DRIVE

S he brought him what she had promised, and they did it in his car, on the top floor of the car park, looking down onto the black flat roofs of buildings, and she said, or she thought she said, "I like your skin," when what she really liked was the color of her father's skin, the mottled white of his arms and the clay color at the roots of the hairs along his arms. Long hair along his arms it was, hair bleached from sun and water—sun off the lake, and all that time he spent in water, summer to summer abrading the wild dry hair on his head, turning the ends of his hair, which was also red, and deeply so, quite white. "You look healthy," she said to her father, and he did, in high color, but the skin on his face also seemed coarse to her—not boy's skin, her father's, not glossy, close-grained skin, but pitted and stubbled under all that

3

color, rashed along his jaw and neck, her father's skin: rough. She touched him, and it was rough skin, his cheek. "Just testing," she said, and smiled at her father. "Shaving," she said. "I used to watch Mother's guys at it."

Her father said, "My youngest daughter still"; then he took hold of her hand and kissed it. He was quiet. Holding her hand against his leg and looking out at a roof where a fat woman waited for her dog, her father was quiet. "What a dirty place this is," he said. "That poor dog is ashamed of himself."

"Look at my hands," she said. "I have seen lots of things," she said, changing the sheets of incontinent patients on rounds made twice a night—all of them up, anyway, these old howlers, mean and balked and full of worry. The naked woman with her pocketbook is crying after baby while the farmer at the nurses' station slaps the counter for a drink. "Where the fuck," the farmer says over and over. "You should know this about me," she said to her father. "I can take care of myself."

"So tell me what you have seen," her father said, and she told him about her mother and the guy with the criminal haircut. "Can you imagine?" she asked her father. Imagine the two of them, inviting her in after, turning over the pillows and fanning at their chests by lifting up the sheet. And there was more, she said, a lot more, but it was her father's turn. "You promised," she said. "The wife."

"The wife," he said.

The wife has see-through skin and grainy eyelids bruised by nature. When she wakes, there is all this sand between her lashes. Daughters, too, there are—brown and knobby daughters, dozens of them, Scotch-taping bangs and walking through the house in their underwear.

She told her father a girl had kissed her once, and not a girl really, but a woman, a teacher, a small, dark, trembly woman who followed all the games at school, running herself breathless up and down the playing field.

''How did it feel,'' her father asked, ''to kiss a woman?''

''I don't remember,'' she said. ''The woman turned teacherly and took me by the shoulders.''

''You are such a show-off,'' T said. ''You are vain. You are braggy.''

She told her father about these girls she knew who were in love with each other. They let her watch them kiss at the lake after swimming. Their kissing was not so dry or hard-seeming as the kissing she remembered with her teacher, and she spoke of the blond abundance of the girl-girl curled outside a high-cut suit; but there was so much smoke in the car by then, she did not know if she imagined the square and heavy ends of her father's fingers, or if she saw or had hold of his fingers, of the whorled dead-white ends of his fingers, tips weighted as surely as a line, deep fishing, plummet of fat in the black-green water—what was that thing he said he caught? Lifted out of the water and beating against her as it had, the fish curling and uncurling in the heat of her hand, did it have a name?

"Tell me about your boyfriends," her father said. Her father asked, "Who else besides the character who gets you this stuff?"

"Just the character," she said, and she called the character T because she didn't want to give him a name. A name could get them all in trouble. "T is just a hairless boy—doesn't need to shave," she said. Same age, but not her size. Smaller, prettier—T had a lean girl's face, sharp angles, good bones. The hammocked skin underneath his eyes fluttered when he kissed. "I look," she said.

Her father kissed her, his dry lips slack against her own and soft. Gentle enough, this time; she could have looked, but she was shy: ready to move in what ways he moved, toward her or away, a lot depending on the things she brought him. That is what she thought at least, that is what she told him, but her father said, "No, no, no."

Her father said, "My problem is, I'm tired."

Another boy, another car, she used to let him feel her up just so long as she could sleep. "The night shift," she said to her father, "is such a bitch. You're always tired. I can't talk," she said, and she kissed her father. She opened her mouth to him and worried her hand inside his coat and felt the warm damp of his shirt, the hard back and heat of her father. Here was no girl-boy, but heavy muscle and bone, soft, wide shoulders and something like breasts. She liked to push against and rub her face between her father's breasts. She rubbed her face in him: lemons and gin and earth and smoke. His springy hair was in her teeth, everywhere springy, and fragrant and wet and tasting of nails. Yes, the metals in my mouth, she said, are singing.

She told T she couldn't remember where she had parked her car.

That was why she was late, she told T. This was another time she couldn't remember. They had driven around and around, she and her father, looking for the street. "Honest," she said, but T didn't believe her, and he put his hand in under her skirt to prove it.

T said, "You are so fucking easy to get at," which she supposed was true, the way she dressed, the way she Velcroed shut, ready to unravel at a tab for a boy—any boy, or that was what T said. "I can see through your dress," T said. "I know what you've been doing."

Under the watchful eye of a man whose name she did not now remember, she took off her skinny bra. He only wanted to look, the man said, and touch her, just a little.

"You would like my mother," she said to the man. "You should see my mother."

"Should I be ashamed?" she asked her father. The lady and her dog were gone; only skin-colored fence acted guardrail on a road: no view.

"Of what?" he asked.

Third party to things, watching, scattering other women's charms like seed and clucking in a backward shuffle was how she saw herself, asking, "Do you like that woman? Did you see her breasts?"

Her father said, "I like your breasts."

Full snub-nosed breasts, nipples tightened to the size of quarters in the cold, she liked these breasts, too, and girls with boy chests and ribs showing through, which wasn't the way she was made, or maybe it was—she wasn't sure, even though she looked when she was being touched. She knew these feelings. The damp press and hurtful weight of a man's head against her collar—beard, no beard—she had known this.

"Everyone else," she told her father, "seems to have what I want."

Her father said, "My daughters are the same." Spoiled girls, they were using Daddy's credit cards to clean beneath their nails, asking, Can we? Why don't we? We should. Her father said, "I don't think of you that way," and he pressed the heel of his hand against her hip as he might to push away, to push off, hard body arched, moving stiffly in the cold waters just off the rocks.

The summer houses were shut up for the winter. November, midday, and the black lake level against the yellow shore. ''We could go there,'' her father said, but they stayed put, in his car, and used the things she brought.

T said, ''Even your mother wants it,'' and she was surprised.

T said, ''Oh, come on, everything you fucking do on that night-shift fucking job is crooked.''

''What do you do,'' she asked her father, ''when you are not with me?''

He said, ''You don't really want to know,'' and he drove her to an unfinished place and pointed. ''I have something to do with that.'' She saw a building, girders, rags, nets, menacing vacancies. Her father pointed. ''Nobody home,'' he said, ''but that's not my job.'' Rocking the car easy over the scrub-board road, raising dust, her father said, ''We'll never get this thing finished.''

Dust settling on the canvased shapes, Dumpsters and cinder block, the whole wild modern array of it—amazing.

''Amazing,'' she said to her father, looking out the window and back at him: the whiteness of his collar against the blaze of neck, the creases darkened, almost black. At his throat, he wore a tie knotted tight as a knuckle.

Maybe he draws the buildings; maybe he warehouses nails and joints, figure-eight pieces, metal supports. Who knows? The way her father palmed the wheel of his fat car, he might very well be a crook with a crook's car, much like an office, plush and neutral, her father's make, coppery glitter and paneling that might or might not be real wood. Black and gold buttons for everything; the music on the radio—never clearer. Only decide, decide, please. You pick, no you, was the way she was with her father, first word always *yes* to everything he asked about. Yes, I did. Yes, I will.

Yes when he surprised her, coming up almost to her house and pointing to a shut eye. "Do you believe my wife did this?" he asked, the good eye blinking and teary and strained. "Can you come out with me for just a while?" Yes.

Yes, Dad: The name warmed her every time she used it to his face, so that she rarely used this name—or any other to his face. Instead, she signaled him. She gave directions in the way she touched him, sometimes saying, "You" and "You" when she was tired and wanted to let him know she would, all he had to do was ask, but not tonight. Tonight she wasn't feeling well.

"But yes," she said to her father. She was always saying yes to her father, and only when she was away from him did she wonder, Does this make sense, my father? Driving all the way to her and home again and to her again in a night, driving to where she worked and waiting for her in the lot until the morning—did her father make sense?

"Twice in a night, it happened," she said to T. "I get confused."

She said, "But I like what I am doing. I wanted to be in something hard. I wanted to be up all night."

"You're so fucking out of it," T said, and all the other boys said, too. "How do you know one man from another?"

The heavy-lidded eyes, the brittle hair and color of her father: first off, these things, and his voice she knew. The juicy sweetness of his voice when her father was drinking, the way even the words came unbuttoned, the way he said her name, she could be done in by this much about him.

Also the money he gave her—and why not?—presents between the covers of oversized matches: *Don't strike* in gold from O' Something's bar.

"Are these from us?" she asked her father, holding up matches. "Have we been here?"

"You," she said, in the car again, free to speak and ready—even her earlobes oiled, every part of her clean and cleaned. She could get off looking at and petting the hair on her arms. "I don't understand," she said. "What are you doing with a wife who beats you?"

"Oh," her father said, and he was sad, or he was tired. Hard to give it up, the look out onto water, someplace to go. Neighbors far apart on either side— not seen until the winter, then sighted in the forked spaces: women standing at windows waiting to be seen. "But it is hard to see them," her father said. "The glare hurts my eyes, and the bog of common plants—the sappy heart-shaped greeny danglers—beads the windows. Nothing happens, besides," he said. "I don't know why the wife is jealous."

She said, "The light in rooms like that puts me to sleep. I know the daughters," she said. From schools and summers, she knew them, diving for soap chips in the boathouse, she and the daughters playing to know what it felt like. The winner held the soap between her legs the longest—oh, yes, she remembered everything about this game. The way it ticked inside of her. "I wanted to melt down soap," she said. "But all of us girls got to play," she said. "We all got to fold our hands over the burning part."

They switched places. Her father tipped the seat and shut his eyes. She said, "I'm my mother's daughter. I want more than others." The way it was for her to wake up in the morning: The reason you think you have been here is you have been here. "I don't want it the same," she said.

"Everyone I know is broke," she said. "The night shift doesn't pay much. My boyfriends never work."

"And your mother?" her father asked when she had already told her stories: grandfather and uncles making house calls on her mother and scolding the poor woman before they made it better, every day less charmed by her mother, opening their wallets, saying, "This has got to stop. There is only so much we can take."

"Do you remember at all? Do you remember her at all?" She said, "Nothing has changed."

Her father said, "I can't get excited when I think about your mother."

"I am shivering," she said, and he was, too. She could see the cold in his shoulders and in her arms resting on his shoulders; and both of them, she and her father, white, blue-white—November still—and the horizon cindered thin, burnt-out, quite black. She put her bare foot against the car door window and said, "Look at my leg." No-color sky, battered grasses. After a while, she asked, "Is this doing anything for you?"

Her father smiled. He said, "I've had better," which made her laugh, his saying, when what did he know?

"Just ask me how many times," she said. "I couldn't tell you."

She said, "I'm always in love with someone."

Her father said he meant it, he was tired, and she put her hands on his face to feel the bristle grown in driving just to get away—a day, a night, another day, as he had said.

"We don't have to do anything," she said.

Her father asked her, "Do you think I look young, or do you think I look like some old guy who got his eyes done cheap?"

"Look at my feet," she said, parked near the boat launch to a lake they didn't know, iced over, gray-white, no clear shoreline. "Look at the footmarks I've left on the window."

"Such white feet," her father said, and he put his foot over hers.

"Have I told you this before?" she asked.

But T didn't answer, bapping pencils against her head and dancing to his made-up music.

Her father said, "Find some music."

"Not that," her father said. "And no to that, no, no"; then he forgot about the music or was indifferent to it; she could stop at anything she liked.

"But do you like it?" she asked her father.

. . .

''Do you like this dress?'' she asked. ''These shoes?''

Her father said, ''It's hard for me to see. My eye still hurts.'' So she drove again, and she told her father what it was as they passed it, and in what connection to him were these women at the end of narrow drives in houses near the water. She spoke of aproned Annes and pretty Susies. ''You knew them,'' she told her father.

Her father said, ''Did I?''

Her father said, ''I don't miss many people.''

She said, ''I don't understand how you can stay with a wife who beats you.'' There, running after her father down the hallway in his story, was a small woman with a small head and a racket in her hand. Why did he stay with this woman? she wanted to know, and he never answered her, or not that she remembered. What could he have answered, besides, married to a woman such as this: marigoldy hair and bright mouth. After all those daughters, the wife still blushed. Some sweet name it was, flicked loose from the roll, a Cathy, a Jane, ring guards clanking on her wedding finger.

She said, ''You should live with me.''

She said, ''Maybe you don't want to know this, but it doesn't take much.'' She was talking numbers—

two and three a week, once that many in a day. "And I'm not very big," she said. "A bigger woman could take more."

"Once, here at the park," she said, driving her father slowly through the main streets of the town, pointing out where she had been. Here, the last time, with some doper—boots and lots of hair—the two of them on the roof, overlooking the entire fucking wayward county. She said, "Oh, Dad, anyone with what we had could have seen everything, too." Mother and one of her guys in her Mustang or her Bronco— the woman turning in cars as fast as she did men— grandfather and the uncles honking close behind. Keep your wallet shut; sign nothing; say you don't speak the language. She said, "What do I care about those guys? They're not looking out for me."

"I know who lives there," she said, and she pointed to insinuating driveways, raked gravel, money. She told her father she was easily coaxed into cars, at times even asking for it, waiting in obvious places for something to happen, in bedrooms and bathrooms, at door-ways with lots of traffic. She said, "I can be dumb sometimes. I don't always know what I am thinking."

Look at the shoes she wore and the dresses.

Mother's mother was still sewing flaps on the cups of the girl's brassieres, so she would look flat, more boy-girl than girl, as if that were going to change things, as if there weren't other ways to do it. "I know lots of ways," she said to her father. "Look," she said, and she lifted up her shirt. "Look at what the lawn did to my back."

She showed her father something else that she had

brought, but he said, "No." Her father said, "I don't feel like it today."

T said, "The shit you deal wears off too fast."

"What do I care?" she said. "There are always men somewhere with money. I've got my grandfather, remember. I've got my uncles."

A friend of a friend had a place for them to go in a big-enough town where a lot went unnoticed, but her father said, "No. I don't feel like it today."

"No," her father said. "No, I have no place to keep it. Just let me kiss you," he said, which she did. Arms crossed and eyes shut tight in the cold of the car, she moved a little closer to him and waited for the blow.

THE SUMMER AFTER
BARBARA CLAFFEY

I once saw a man hook a walking stick around a woman's neck. This was at night, from my mother's window. The man dropped the crooked end behind the woman's neck and yanked just hard enough to get the woman walking to the car. I saw this and saw rain winking in the yard in the light around our house.

Our house has the streetlight.

Mother says, "Our house marks the start of this corny town," and the two of us laugh at what it takes to be the start of something.

Here is the house at night, lit up tall and tallowy. And in the morning, here is Mother, first one up by hours and already in a swimsuit and weeding muddy beds on her hands and knees. She has mud on her back and in her hair, and streaks have dried behind an ear where Mother says she has been scratching. Her arms are scored with bleeding cuts, nails mud-dull and broken, and there are mean-looking bites on her back, white swellings she must not feel or will not yet give in to touching, brave as Mother says she is to get hold of what she wants. I have seen shaggy weed ends spooled around my mother's hand rope-tight. "But look," she says, and wags off dirt from balled-up roots the size of shrunken heads.

This is what I have found to show Mother from the garden: one of a pair, dime-store flip-flops, size large.

Mother frowns at it. "Not his," she says. "This last Jack didn't have feet."

"Garbage, then," I say, like all my other finds— an upper plate of teeth, scarves, umbrellas, pens, and once, in the middle of the driveway, a ruined shirt so flattened by the weight of cars driving over and over, it had taken on the shape of a dead thing, and I had carried it to Mother on a stick.

Mother is still on this last Jack and on all the things about him that were missing. "For that matter," she says, "this last Jack didn't have hands." She says this with her hands under cold water, cutting off the ends of flowers. One end pellets off the wall, then rolls under the kitchen table. I watch where it goes, but I will not pick that up, please.

No, Mother.

No telling the things under there—oily tacks and combs, bread crusts and withered peas, always more, and furred with such a dust that I think they come alive at night and breed.

Mother says, "Don't be such a ninny. Go and get it."

But no amount of teasing will send me looking for the bits of flowers that fly out in her wild cutting.

"You put your scissors up too high," I tell my mother.

I tell her something else she may or may not know: how we used to stand in line for it, me and Barbara Claffey, shivering in our new bodies and waiting our turn for instruction. Barbara Claffey swore the last Jack used his tongue.

Mother doesn't believe this story. "So where was I?" she asks.

"Chawed grass," I say. "That's how he tasted."

Mother smiles at me. "Just be glad you were there," she says. "You are probably smarter for it."

In and out of doors, I slug around the morning in my baby-dolls. I have nothing to hide, I tell my mother, although I don't know what to play with anymore.

Mother says, "Bored, bored, what's to be bored about?" and she moves from room to room, hitching rolled papers under her arm, clucking glasses in a grip—two, three, swiped off her bedside table in a motion. She uses water on the table and her nails to get up bottle rings of cough syrup that she says help when she can't sleep. Snaking the vacuum under her bed, Mother snorts up Kleenex. "Last night was bad. Coughing," she says, "and coughing."

"I didn't hear a thing," I say. Right through the

streetlight's sudden extinction, the house went on sleeping with me.

Mother on her hands and knees, in the garden, is what I wake to, day after day, pressed out of doors by the midsummer heat rising in the houses of this hokey town. The Smiths across the street, the Dunphies next door, all the way to the end of the road—in what Mother calls a farm and Barbara Claffey calls a subdivision—are neighbors dressed in scant disguises. Too white, Mother says, or too fat for these clothes, but they don't know any better. Mother calls our neighbors hicks and winces when she sees Junior Klenk cut through our yard. Ready for a girl, she says, if he knew what to do with one.

Like that last Jack—he knew. Yipping the way he did that time in the yard when I saw him pricking Mother's legs with a weenie fork.

"Not mine," Mother says. "Some twangy girl's from someplace south. Watch out!" Mother warns. "The girls down there are dumb as foxes."

I think of us, me and my mother in this nowhere town, in the flattened middle of the country. What do we know?

Barbara Claffey knows how to wad a pair of socks into bundles tight as baseballs.

"But does she know how to kiss?" Mother asks, shuffling through bills and bills and more bills, saying, "This is what I have to do now. I have to figure out how to pay for things."

. . .

I have to do nothing. Nothing, nothing long into the afternoon with the morning just-remembered light rising in her room.

''No reason to panic,'' is what Mother says, and she looks over her shoulder as if expecting trouble, when all I want to know is, What is there to do? ''I've left things for dinner,'' Mother says, and takes up her glass and makes like this is coffee she is drinking, and she, a busy lady, elbowing the fridge, on the run, no time to talk, when she is talking all the time to friends in other, smarter towns. I sit between my mother's legs with my shirt hitched to my shoulders. ''Scratch,'' I say. This way, I don't mind when it is phone, phone, phone. This way, there is company.

''The tomatoes are alive,'' I say, in the kitchen again, worrying about my dinner. I lift off foiled lids to things she should have thrown away: jellied gravy, old rice.

''I can guess what you're thinking,'' Mother says, ''but all that Barbara Claffey could do was fold cubed fruit in Jell-O.''

I know how to mix drinks and make good scrambled eggs, buttery and smooth and not overstirred.

I know how to use a phone if I can recall a number.

''But there is never any paper,'' I say. ''And where are all the pencils?'' Not like when the last Jack was here and bringing home thc pens he said he stole from office girls. Big on where to put things, that Jack, left and right, above, below. The boxed cuff links, the money clips, the sized and guttered coins at the front of the drawer he shared with Mother.

The last Jack was particular even to the way he ate. "Remember?" I ask her. I used to pester him about the melon rinds he left scooped smooth as boat keels, or the ears of corn with each pocket emptied yet unbroken and erect. How did anyone eat corn, I wanted to know, so that the cobs, stacked four- and five high on the plate, looked like something you could eat again?

"Oh, Jack," Mother says. "His problem was he didn't drink enough."

"And his handwriting," I say, and Mother scowls at me. She does not remember his lists of what he left for us to do. The dashing caps on his capitals or the evenness of his hand, word by word, line by line, on unlined paper. Only business, that Jack said.

The white in his hair—why, white paint, what else? And the red in his eyes, just red string. I believed him.

Mother says, "He only looked like some big deal."

Under the kitchen table, I licked this Jack's plump shoes, both. But neither tasted of anything I knew of.

"Look," Mother says, and I can see her looking out from the crack in the door she leaves open when she pees. "You can always lock the door."

My mother soaping her throat is what I hear, and soaping the ledge along her throat where she sometimes lays her hand when she is quiet.

"This is the plan," she is saying. "Someone hand-some is on his way here. His name is John," my mother says, "but we know what that means."

Black hair, I think, buzzed to a shadow at the back of the neck.

"This new Jack is different," Mother says. "This new Jack has some style. Not like the last Jack with his surf and turf or turf and surf—whatever the shit, on your first night out. Here's style for you, the last Jack's idea: snifters of candy on every table. What a dunce!" Mother says, handing me her puff and pow-der, showing me her back.

I white out trails of water leaking from her snarled hair.

"I know about a lot of things," Mother is saying, "but I do not know about men. Only this," Mother says, stepping from the damp and powder-traced impressions of her feet. "This last Jack had no taste. This last," Mother says, "I dressed him. Remember the suits?"

I remember coats, gray and odorless, square-cut and severe—the same, the same, shrilling on the closet rod.

"The cashmere sweaters?" Mother says. "In case he read a book."

I remember hats—not stiff, not Grandfather's hats, those upside-down coffins, but soft hats slumped at ease.

"Jack and his affable act," Mother says. "But he was handsome," Mother says. "I got carried away."

All those ties my mother bought him—so many, a ladderwork contraption looped with ties, one over another, sometimes slipping loose, falling in a faint behind the shoe racks. I have found these ties in the back of Jack's closet and used a broom handle on them.

"Do you have to go out?" I ask Mother, and I follow her from room to room.

"I have to think," Mother says, putting on her model's coat, looking through her closet. Dressing for this new Jack as she did for all the others takes up lots of time, she says. The purses packed like eggs, the mixed-up shoes all hooked in sacks.

"Better to be small," Mother says, taking out her slimming skirt. "Men take care of small women."

But I may grow to be as big as Mother. I have her hair, and what I think were once her eyebrows.

"And the rest?"

Mother smiles at me. "Takes two," she says.

I do not have my mother's face—that much I know. I do not have the face my mother wears for all her Jacks, smooth and lit-up and amazed. Beautiful, the Jacks all say, and she is. I have seen women stop to look at her, my mother, and sometimes even ask, Have they seen her before? Have they seen this face in magazines, the same face my mother pulls at now, pinching up her eyelids, saying, "I may be too old for this business."

"So why do you want to go?" I ask, watching the light wash over Mother's laid-out clothes. Slip, panties, pearls, and dress, all the whites turned old-teeth yellow.

''What do you think?'' Mother asks, pouting at the mirror.

I say, ''I think you shouldn't wear that dress. And don't let this John know you have any money.''

Mother says, ''Okay, little mother. What should I wear?''

''I don't know,'' I say. ''Just stay buttoned. And don't tell this guy about me,'' I say.

Mother says, ''I'm not listening to you.''

''Remember the last Jack?'' I ask.

''Oh that bastard,'' she says, ''but what do you think he was doing to me?'' She is penciling eyebrows, arched and alert. ''Yes?'' Mother asks. ''I'm waiting,'' and she rubs off an eyebrow in the harsh way she did when this last Jack was here and she was always washing, saying she smelled bad—and Mother did not smell bad.

Night after night, dinner on the porch at the glass-topped table, me between the two of them, this last Jack and Mother, I sometimes got the smell of her confused with food and snatched her wound-up lip-stick once and bit her red in half. I remember.

Under the glass-topped table, I saw my mother's long brown legs crossed at the ankles, thucking her heel in and out of her shoe.

'' 'Do you think everything you do is so pretty?' this last Jack said.''

I ask, ''What did he mean by that?''

''Who cares?'' Mother says. ''He made me feel

dirty, that Jack." She licks a paintbrush to a point and outlines her mouth. Mother says, "Oh God, I have no taste in men. Do you know what that means?"

I think.

I think I do—hearing how it was when this last Jack came home. The plak-plak of his briefcase, open and shut; no other word for days.

Mother says, "He was not nice, that Jack."

I say, "So why are you going out?"

"Because I am," Mother says.

And she is standing now, my mother, in the spatter of her dress—back, forth, back, forth—a sweater, a purse, an umbrella in case. "Besides, I am hungry," Mother says, "for surf and turf—who cares? I won't be paying for this stupid meal, and if the man has any manners, I won't know the price."

"Oh, don't go," I say.

She is watching from her window the man's approach across the lawn. "You can wave from here," Mother says in the voice she uses with the new Jacks, and I do.

I wave and wave, even though she is not looking. I wave at my mother muscling her own weight under this Jack's arm. I cannot hear what they are saying; it is quiet in this town.

But the neighbors must notice my mother and her Jack. Either side of us and across the street, the Dunphies, the Smiths, Barbara Claffey down the street, must press to windows startled as by birds that swoop and mate so queerly close. I sometimes draw the blinds to them—but not to Mother. I am ready for Mother and her sudden turning to see if I am watching her, to see if I am paying attention to how she stands, tottering in her shoes, ankles gagged and tense and helpless—and Mother is not helpless. My mother is brave, I think, and her upturned face is shining. I see this, and see them both, willful lovers, tilted away from the house, leaning hard into the night.

WHAT HAVE YOU BEEN DOING?

S he was out of practice, and he wanted practice, so they started kissing each other, and they called it practicing, this kissing that occurred to him. In the middle of rooms, she obliged, in her bedroom, his bedroom, a kissing done standing, her hands on his shoulders, his not quite on her waist, heads tilted, mouths open. "Like this?" the boy asked, and the mother said, "Yes," but kept her tongue to herself, and only laughed sometimes at the suddenness of his—his tongue that in its darting seemed not his. The way he drew back to laugh and to ask, "Isn't that right?" made her think he didn't like that part, not quite, not the way she liked that part and how it was he tasted—always he tasted of a warm sweet water, and of a breath so clean, she wondered how she must have tasted, so that she shut her mouth to him and steered him by the shoul-

3 1

ders to his desk or to his bed and said, "Okay, you know now." She said, "Someday you will make a girl happy," and her saying so made the boy smile, for this was something the boy wanted to do—he was in training, she knew, in readiness for making a girl happy.

He said, "I am going to have a maid when I grow up." They were in the kitchen then, the boy and the mother, rinsing dishes. "Lucky you," she said, and they went on washing dishes.

"I am going to have three houses," the boy said. This was later, another time. "I don't know where," the boy said. "But the places will be important." The mother was approving and asked what she always asked: "May I visit?"

"If Dad is not there," the boy answered, and later, another time—for these ideas, she found, came to him as suddenly as kissing—he said, "I will have houses for you next to all of my houses."

Sometimes the boy thought of dancing. He put on his music and called out to the mother, "Come dance," and she went to the boy because she knew the music—she told him so. "This was our music," the mother said, "before you were born." She taught the boy how to stroll and cakewalk and guide a girl under the arch of his arm. She told him, "The girls love boys who love to dance," and "The girls love boys who ask." When she told the boy these things, she put her arms around his neck and swayed, pulling on his slow, sleepy body, his big feet hardly moving, his hands at his sides—his boneless, dimpled child hands cupped and open and cool to her touch. She pressed to find his knuckles, to measure, by feeling the length of his fingers, which, she believed, was a measure of the man to be, or was it feet? She could never remember—but his fingers were short and his thumbnail, when she looked, was rucked and milky. "Bad boy," she said, and she put his thumb in her mouth and tongued the whorled thumb pad. "Okay," the boy said, "I get the idea," and he pulled away from her embrace and started his own dance, a made-up dance, hop-skipping to his room. "I want to play now," the boy called. "And can you get me something to eat?"

She was in the bathroom, and he was at the door. Mornings, evenings. "Do you mind?" she answered. "Are you deaf?" she asked, pressing a wet washcloth over her breasts and turning away from the cold huff of air in the door's opening. "Just checking," the boy said—and the mother smiled when she shouted, "I have no privacy here!"

Room to room, stacked straight, tight, divisions so thin she could hear the boy at night butting against the wall between her bedroom and his. She thought of horses knocking in their stalls and wondered was it the boy's foot or out-thrown arm, and would he, in some half sleep, come to her, shuffling on his big feet, saying, "I brought my own pillow." She was always awake when he came to her and remembering what not to forget, so that to have this boy next to her, the sidelong press of him on his back, arms crossed over his chest, a sealed package to poke and wonder at, was a way of remembering, and she thought, This cannot be bad—and she sometimes spent the night with him.

"You didn't move!" was what the boy said, finding

his mother when he did not expect to find her in the morning still beside him, but in his own bed and explaining, "You take up all the room," or saying, "Here is room," and smoothing the place beside her.

Awake like this and in bed together, there was often nothing left to say, and so they kissed. They kissed as boys and mothers kiss: she, dry smacking everywhere fast—cheek, nose, chin, neck—and he, giddy in the heat of her kissing, kissing back slow and wet and opening his shirt to let her scratch. "Here," he said, "and here," pointing to low places prickling at her touch, pointing lower.

"You!" the mother said, and roused herself from his bed. "You must be hungry," she said.

In this way, the day began, or else it happened he was gone, and she was in his bed "Because the light was better," she said, and the pillows, plumped so near the window, stayed cool. And if the phone rang, very early, as it did when he was gone, she was nearer to it, ready to answer in a wide-awake voice, knowing even before he spoke, it was the boy calling. He was as suddenly moved to call her as he was to kiss her, and with nothing more on his mind than "What have you been doing, what are you doing now?"

"Braiding corn tassels," the mother said. "Gouging eyes in the potatoes."

The boy, at home again, said, "I am going to have lots of children."

The boy said, "I will never get divorced."

The boy was locking himself in the bathroom then. He was saying, "I want privacy." He was saying, "Look at me"—goose-stepping toward the mother, naked as the day he was born, and asking, ''Who am I?'' The boy's game—''Who am I now?''

''A soldier,'' the mother said.

''A bad man,'' the mother said.

But she could never guess him right.

The boy changed even as the mother answered, coming at her in some goofy bump and grind. She looked, and then she did not look, and swiped at his soft belly, and swiped again to keep him back, and when he kept on jiggling toward her, she took hold of his shoulders until he stood still and away from her, but not so far she could not touch him. She pressed her thumbs against his pink squint-eyed nipples, and the boy said, ''You are my mother.''

The mother said, ''So?''

''One kiss.''

And the boy gave it to her, fast, before he moved away from where the mother was standing, in the middle of a room she did not recognize, in a body that was suddenly not quite hers.

GOOD NIGHT,
SWEETHEART

I date an old man, a man so old, I am afraid to see what he is like under his clothes. I am afraid of his old mouth and his old breath. His eyes, when he looks at me, are watery and sad, even when he is laughing, and he is often laughing, just behind me, at a joke I have made. This old man seems to like me. He takes me to dinner; he lets me talk and talk, like boys used to do. My mouth waters with the pleasure of it, telling stories whole, being heard; I order dessert; I flirt. All this heat hatches my face. I feel it, and I am happy, schoolgirl happy, with a man I am afraid to kiss.

I have done my share of kissing—so what am I afraid of? The teeth, their leafy transparency? His teeth remind me of my grandfather's teeth, and the shock, up close, of all that metal inside his mouth.

I never talk to the old man about my grandfather.

My past reads earnest as a yearbook; I mostly keep it to myself. We have an understanding, the old man and I—he keeps the talk since the last wife's death. Always, he pays for dinner.

I like watching him take out his wallet. He seems very shrewd to me when he takes out his wallet—on his own, no need of me. I can get excited; I admit it. He looks good to me then. His brick red neck, his grizzle—a kind of overgrown look he has—hair in the ears and growing over even the knuckles, I am attracted to this about him, and especially to his knuckles, his hands. His hands are brown and easeful; I want to touch them. So why is it, when he touches me, I flinch?

I worry when the meal is over.

I worry about the walk home.

What does he expect?

His face blurs and tires; there is no sign of wanting, none that I can read. Used to be the body knew; the body made the decisions. I could smell it, all that want, and I knew what to do. The awkwardnesses—putting on a coat, taking up my purse—were only felt as tweaks on the way to the next event. The point was to leave— never as it is now: to wait, to consider. The point was move fast, get home, get anywhere.

Outdoors, indoors, rooms—all rooms—once even on a porch to a house I was helping christen: It happened anywhere, sometimes even with restrictions, insurmountable now, so drunk or dopey, the room turned to fuzz. I had sex when I was tripping, when I was sick with the flu, and often in the middle of my bleeding with so much coming out of me, I should have been embarrassed, not as I was, indifferent to precautions and towels, staining the bed, me, him, seeing his mouth red, but I cannot see this old man's mouth ever being red.

His age bleaches even his past.

I cannot see this man's mouth at all.

He has pinched up his muffler. We are walking against the wind around the building where I live. The building is dark; even the doorman is absent. No one is waiting up for me.

RELIGION

We woke in the parked car aslant in the field Cory's grandma had found for us to sleep in, turned earth in front of us, almost houses behind, frames and unpoured sidewalks, abandoned machines and wheelbarrows left anywhere in the thin light that was the afternoon light we knew for spring in the county. We had lived through these long, wrong seasons before; we knew this cold, how even the fruit trees went on pouting, unwilling as girls to unfurl their crimped leaves, show their blossoms. Too cold to have even unrolled the windows before we fell asleep—on the instant—the car driving itself over the ridged site and tender, penned-off, seeded yards to settle safely at an angle on higher ground.

Here it was, awake again, we hushed the unmade house that we had left behind, the sorrowful impres-

sions of bodies in beds, blankets, curtains, clothes
bunched and flung away, my sister's crying when what
was there worth crying about?

"Did you want to go on peeing in a pan in the
basement," we asked my sister, "no running water?"
Food greasing the goosenecked paper bags the women
gave us for the afternoon when they remembered there
would be an afternoon with us children left to draw
in the common room; nothing but gobby pens and
squared-off pencils sharpened by a knife to make our
names with—we used erasers. We could blow off what
we wrote: our names and our mothers' names and
where we had come from or been to, which was no
place you would want to be once you had learned how
to spell it.

But the stuttering boy, he couldn't even say where
it was he had been to. Lemon-water yellow color of
someone sickly, he slunk about the compound, brushing his hand across his brush-cut hair, worrying his
father's dying in that *tuh-town* he couldn't say—his
mother in the bleeding room with our mothers, keeping clean.

"Do you remember at all?" we asked my sister,
who did not answer and might still have been sleeping
when we were in the front seat saying, "Yes, it was a
good thing we had left our mothers—who knew what
they were doing?"

Kneading his feet with their spatulate thumbs,
salving the raised skin of wounds.

"How he suffers!" they said, walking among us
with his terrible vision when the grasses shudder on an
intake of breath and cattle list, and all things roosting or

rooting lift off, move away, flame on flame taking up the field and us—but not by name. This man named Jerry, he was not always sure of our names. Jerry called us after others, or else it was we were the children, although I was no child. I had been to the bleeding room. I knew what the mothers inside were doing, washing one another and applying hot waxes. Three, four, five days shut off, standing in the steam of the herbal boil, we came out clean and nearly hairless, our knuckles pinked from scrubbing rags with stones.

The compound was so primitive. There was a spigot in the greenhouse where the shot-out panes were taped with plastic, moaning in the wind. We made the stuttering boy or the older Ruth go there to the greenhouse—"Although it could have been you," we told my sister. "Would you have liked that, the florist spikes and prickly markers at your feet, talking to the spigot, saying, Hurry, please, hurry?"

We did not like to be alone on the compound, but we were often alone on the compound with the babies in sodden diapers, licking dirt. My sister found a dead rat and thought it was a kitten and came carrying it back to us in tears. We beat the dead rat with a shovel. We beat Naomi, too. We each took a whack at that stalk of a girl, running in the heat in just her underpants. The oppressive summers in this county—you need some way to stay cool.

"Don't you want air conditioning?" we asked the baby, my sister. "Don't you like the comforts in this car?"

"I miss Mother," was what my sister said. "I want to go back."

But we told Cory's grandma, "Don't pay attention to her. She doesn't know what she is saying. Drive on, please," which she did, with Cory wheezing again in the front seat, and Cory's grandma asking, "Where's that thing you suck on, Coreen? Was there no one in that place to think of you?"

No one, no one, we assured her, with the mothers stapling pamphlets and driving to the mall. They looked like messy girls to us, and I was surprised at my mother. She let her hair grow lank and her wide-slung self swing free. She jostled underneath her clothes when she walked, hoisting herself into the cab of the truck, never turning, as some others turned, to wave good-bye.

"Is that your idea of loving?" I asked the sniveler, the baby, my sister.

The mission was *stu-stupid* was what the stuttering boy always said, worrying his real father was already dead in his bed up north where the stuttering boy had seen him. The stuttering boy had said his good-byes before his mother put herself and him in that same truck as ours, had boarded and ridden to the compound, ridden to the mall, ridden to the old towns strung with bunting on the holidays.

Our mothers, butting tambourines and crying out, "Amen!" and crying sometimes—oh, we were embarrassed!

"Weren't you embarrassed?" we asked my sister, which was a feeling she didn't understand, I think, wearing her mopey face, saying, "I liked dancing with Mother. We put cracks in the ceiling from our dancing.

Mother showed me the damage,'' my sister said, and she was crying again, but we weren't embarrassed this time—only angry.

''Drive faster, please,'' we said to Cory's grandma. ''We are too many in this car. It is hard to breathe.''

Under the driver's thumb, all the windows hummed down at once.

''Air!'' we said, and breathed.

Scabs in the spring air on the compound, cotton-seed and petals, early bees and trembling webs, dews, worms, some stones in the sun already warm against our feet—remember spring there? How Jerry caught us in our nightgowns, how he stared? I was ashamed— we all were. We never went outdoors again quite so undressed.

Summer, the last, the insects hung in the air unmoved, the fine threads of their legs just a riffle. We went looking for water beyond the fields, broke through pokered plants to the mud bank, wet-bark brown that was a river. There, crouched, we spit white spit to watch the fish puck at the surface to eat it. I was next to the older boy, the one we never asked to come along but who sometimes came along, took his pants off, made to swim. The older boy dangled his martyred feet in the river. I watched them drift in the sluggish current and saw, too, the dark sacs of his sex, legs apart, water to his knees. Unmuscled arms and narrow shoulders, tender neck and skull, near bald he was, that older boy, ghostly border over nuded ears. We knew which mother had done that to him—and she in tears. But the older boy was a dirty boy; we saw that much about him. Chewed-up lips and blood stars on his cheeks from scratching, the older boy was angry. We were right to leave him.

Cory's grandma said, "Not if I had had more room in this car. If I had had more room in this car, I would have gathered up all of you children."

Jerry used to say things like that, too. On a painfully bright day, when I remembered I might otherwise be in school, I stood—we all stood—at the bleached field under a dark blue sky and listened to him loving us: surcease and promise. Jerry's throat tightened when he spoke, and he unbuttoned his shirt, and we saw the flushed and grizzled heart he beat when he was speaking to us as Jerry was speaking to us. Children, he said, and we were all children—even the mothers— we belonged to him, which was belonging to something more than to a man.

"What are you crying about, you baby, you sister? You didn't even understand what he was saying. You were winding yourself in Mother's skirt. You said you were cold; you said you couldn't see," I said, although we all had to admit it was hard to see him with his back to the sun and our own eyes dazzled from wherever in the sky the sun was shining. Jerry was just a cutout; even his face was black, and his hair, wet slash in his pacing, water dripping off his chin—we never knew a man could dribble as though he were a spigot you could drink from.

I wanted to be his favorite, but when it seemed I might be, I grew afraid of Jerry's snouty fingers sniffing in the dark, his gentling, "You, is this you? Have you been waiting?"

"Oh, I am glad you children wrote me," Cory's

grandma said, and we said we were glad, too. The winter had been hard. Cindered mouth and blank dawning, we slept near to fires and woke, crying, ''Water!'' running after it to the greenhouse with a jar, jumping over babies, their puckered hands smudged black. We wouldn't touch them, though the mothers stomped and cried out, ''Will you take that baby with you!'' But we were after water, running over frozen earth in the fossilized boot tracks of someone's earlier departing in a thaw, in a hurry—other mothers it had been, not ours. Ours were in the common room, waiting for water. They were waiting for Jerry's instructions: what to do next.

Sell your plated silver; close your thin accounts.

''Don't you remember our first house?'' I asked my sister. Father's indentations in the soft couch not yet cold, and already on the curb that Jerry.

''But I liked him,'' my sister said. ''I was carried when I didn't want to walk. He promised he would show me things outside the county.''

''Jerry had nothing in his pockets for us,'' we said. ''His hands were empty and hairless.''

''Soft,'' my sister said, ''warm.''

''Moist, maybe,'' the fingernails cracked, stained. I remembered, too, the fingertips steepled, pressed against his lips as he considered what to do with the stuttering boy when the stuttering boy cried at the table, his face a leaky sore at the mention of a father—anyone's father—when his was dying, was probably dead. ''I thought you were grown up,'' is what Jerry had said, before he took him to the greenhouse and left him bleedy at the spigot.

Cory's grandma said, "Lordy, Coreen, where was your mother in all of this? How was it this Jerry had such a hold?"

"The mothers were easy," we said. They only wanted a word—a *sweetheart* or a *honey*.

The mothers said Jerry's gentleness reminded them of fathers who had had to do hard things for which they yet seemed sorry.

But the man we're talking about was never sorry. Jerry backed up over the older boy's old dog and left the bitch for us to bury. He took the money that our grandparents sent—it was lucky someone knew how to sneak us a stamp!

"Lordy," Cory's grandma said, "lucky!"

"It was lucky you came," we said, when at the windows Jerry said he saw faces—but looking in on what? Mothers putting waxy sacks of white bread on the table, sticks of softened butter? The babies in the common room were licking the TV while the in betweens were slunk on bunk beds, playing who will you marry and what will you be. Not a lot to look in on, although we hoped someone was looking in on the stuttering boy with his mouth taped shut, so that his sound was all blurred howling—and that to rouse his mother from what the man had done to her when she had said, "But Jerry, the boy only wants to see his father before the man is dead."

We said to Cory's grandma, "We knew our letter to you could mean trouble, and we kept some children out of it. We didn't want anyone hurt."

"Do you understand," we asked my sister, "we made some sacrifices. Not everyone is here, you'll notice. Some are missing.'' Some are in the greenhouse still, ripping sheets to strips to stuff the holes with, stop the moaning. The piss pot in the basement, the slops beneath the sink, some child is there, too, cleaning and sweeping the way he had us do to cover the boot tracks and clean the greenhouse of the flowers stood on end, their ganglia of dark roots wire-stiff, their leaves dissolving.

''Have you forgotten,'' we asked my sister, ''those others we left to their suffering?'' The stuttering boy and his bleeding tongue, Naomi with her bruises were only some of what we left behind. There were babies and crawlers, children after mothers, mothers far away if it is mall day—remember? ''Remember them?'' Fluttering inky dittos, the mothers wander malls, seeking others like themselves. What is it that brought us here, they may wonder, but the vacant face in the darkened window, the one we saw in passing and had to claim as ours?

''Those mothers sound drugged,'' Cory's grandma said.

Sometimes, yes, they moved that way. In the river, after standing an eternity cut off at the ankles, they walked—dared to walk—along the shallow stony bottom, moving as mystics move with feet turned out over nails or coals; when pierced by some sharpness or benumbed by the cold, the mothers kneeled into the water and swam out. White necks and weedy hair on these mothers who squealed in the open air, sharing worn soaps and saying, ''Doesn't this feel good after such a winter?''

''Stop crying!'' I said to my sister. ''You and your

tears—you sticky baby, you aren't the only one who misses Mother."

"Of course," said Cory's grandma, "but see here," and she pointed to the streaked trees outside the car windows. "Look, children, what we are coming to!" Tasseled shrubbery and ragged bibs of lawn, snow shovels on front porches, narrowing blocks, less green and higher buildings, chips of colored light blinking on for evening—and us driving into it. April this was, mid-April, May, when the cold rains kept the earth black, before anything could burn.

DEAD MEN

There is a man on top of her up on the top of the bed, and there is a man under her down under the bed, but the man down there is dead. Some years dead and still in the phone book, the dead man under the bed is wrapped in canvas, skull-colored, brown and freckled, though he is not changed, this same long man—caved-in chest, enormous shoes. She will not polish them and wonders can the man on top of her up on the top of the bed see the dead man's shoes— and if he can see them? If the man on top of her— she has no name for him—can see any part of the dead man peeking through, will he stop doing what he is doing to her? Because she likes what he is doing, the man on top of her—call him lover, he is so new to her and taken up in such a hurry, she does not know his name yet—she likes the way his hands move over her, curious and knowing that here is a spot, and here. "Yes," she says, and no one has been right here for a while, so this feels very good, this hand between her legs—forget the dead man.

The lover is good, shucking the split part of her, using his thumb. His hands are cupped for this work; the ready ends of his licked fingers worry deep.

The dead man's fingers are dry; the dead man is a dunce, waiting and sullen. She has to do it for him, the dead man, but not for the lover.

The lover's mouth glistens when he asks, "Can I look?" and he looks at how she is before he puts his lips to her again. He uses his teeth, and when he looks up at her from between her legs, she sees his lips are swollen.

What a wonder—and she likes him here on the bed, the lover, but his feet are over the side of the bed, and she thinks he might inch off the bed to do other things to her on his knees. He might; he might even now be moving nearer to the dead man and the dead man's things under the bed.

"Oh," she says, thinking of those things the lover might dig out—used, dull objects belonging to the dead man—when what she wants to want is what the lover has, which is only himself, and the way he is coaxing her with his tongue.

Before the dead man, she had slept by herself with her hands to herself like a poultice.

Easy to play nasty then with the dead man not quite dead but ashing ash on his bare chest and picking at his teeth with any envelope: windowed bills and notices, heavy paper—ominous address—a letter from her mother asking, "Will you tell me, please, what are you doing with this man?" Printed invitations or credit cards—the dead man made a blade of anything. And she never said, Don't do that. That is not very nice— not very polite. She watched—she watched the dead man clip his nails into last night's coffee and found bleedy streaks on his pillow—but not now; no streaks on the pillow she uses with the lover.

"Here," says the lover, and under her back he stuffs the pillow, which is clean—no sign of the dead man. "Here," he says, and uses his fingers. Even to be grazed here by the lover asking, "Yes?" and she saying, "Yes" is exciting—does he know that? Does the lover know what a tease he is lifted on his arms and knees and swishing his swishy sex, until she says, "I am jealous of it," and she takes hold of him, and they watch his rising over the nest of her.

With the dead man, there is no looking.

"Yes," she says, turning over, tucking under the dead man's pillow and never telling about the dead man, and how it is to wag him feetfirst out from under the bed, thumping the pillow at his back, and then unpacking him, pulling away the canvas—pretending.

She is tired of thinking about the dead man.

But she can see, or thinks she can see, parts of the dead man peeking out from under the bed—his shoes, the breathing canvas—so that it is not the lover but the dead man she is waiting for, his icy lubricants, his long reach for hard objects, his saying, "You could take my fist, you cunt."

And she is all mouth, it is true—a wanting of shameful proportions—not even the dead man's shoe will do, and the lover, she thinks, must know this. His touch already is exhausted, small and dry. Under the bed, she thinks, the sack is still there with its unwashed objects, and the lover might find and use them.

"Do that," she says. "I like what you are doing," and she does, but at this angle, from over the side of the bed, she can see the dead man or what is covering the dead man. The heavy buckled canvas catching on the bed's jostling, she hears it catching and puts her hand out as if to press the dead man still when he is forever making noises—gaseous exhalations in the downward drift.

The dead man always said he was dying.

Yet the lover is alive; the lover is well and moving against her in the half-dark room that is her own again. Only under the bed are things belonging to the dead man—his sack of gadgets, his ledger book of checks. There are golf tees yet in his pocket, although the dead man did not play; the dead man was deadly serious about what things cost and meant in ways, it seems to her, the lover does not know. The lover, she thinks, does not know or want to say he knows what she is—a sore, a hole, a blankness he must try to strike.

The lover says, "I can't do what it is you want me to do."

"Take anything you can find," she says. "Anything off the table," she says, thinking of the tissue box with boxy edges—something not so soft as this lover is soft—and she wonders should she tell him; she wants to tell him about the dead man. He should fucking well know that there is nothing he can do but she would, could, take it.

DAYWORK

We enter the attic at the same time, which makes it all the more some awful heaven here, cottony hot and burnished and oddly bare except for her appliances, the parts our mother used to raise herself from bed. Here they are tilted against the attic walls: the legs, the arms, the clamshell she wore instead of a spine. Here is some of Mother leaned up in the attic.

"We shouldn't be in this room," my sister says. "She isn't dead."

I agree; we might be too much in a hurry taking Mother's house apart. "Mother could get well again," I say, unhooking hangers, finding some of what our mother wore for hair.

"I wouldn't touch it," my sister says. "Don't look."

But we look and look at how the blistered skins of covered bins and clothes bags have gone yellow.

My sister says, "It feels as if someone is watching."
And she opens a long box—but whose, we don't know.

"I'm glad it's you doing that," I say as she sniffs
what looks like gauze, rusty in places, violently stained.

"Little worms," she says. "I'm not kidding."

"Throw it out," I say, waving away what things
my sister brings me. The netting and the tape and the
wired sheets—what good are these to us or anyone?
I sling a fat sack down the attic stairs to pile with the
others. Dark bags full of Mother's house—so much we
don't know what to do with we throw out: old clothes
cut to fit over the parts that Mother buckled on.

"This stuff, too?" my sister asks. She is looking at
the hinged machinery hooked on the attic walls: a cane
with teeth, a bedside pull, a toilet seat with armrests.

"Pile it," I say, wondering who would ever choose
to use and save such things? Who would sit behind a
flimsy screen attended to and cleaned while visitors
made shadows on the other side? The low-pitched *Oh*
embrace of it, the pain we have heard, and how our
mother talked to it, talked about it, showing off her
bruises, saying, "They don't know where to stick me
anymore. They can't find a vein," or saying, "Look at
what they've done to me," or saying, "Remember, will
you, visit."

One of the visitors, I have heard our mother easing
into sleep and whispering to nurses, "Lover."

"Why did she let them do it?" I ask my sister, but
my sister says she doesn't know.

My sister asks, "Did you see these?" And she holds
out spongy socks meant to pass as shoes. "What about
these?"

"Oh, Mother never liked to walk," I say.

Lately, she gives up in the middle of a sentence. Mother fades away and chews her gum against the mouthpiece of the phone. There is all this fuzz between us; "I don't belong here," Mother says, to which I don't know what to say.

You will never get any better, Mother?

You should wish yourself dead?

We make such terrible confessions, my sister and I, which is why we are uneasy in the attic in the presence of these parts of Mother that seem a part of her still, quite alive and listening in on what we talk about. The way our mother lets herself be seen getting in and out of beds—the stained lips, the patched-on nipples from when her breasts had seams and looked shut as drawstring purses.

Purses, there are none here in the attic, only overnight bags fitted with zippers to expand and expand for Mother's longer visits, months spent in hospitals, listening to the *pling, pling* of some necessity—nurse, elevator, doctor, dear! What does Mother want? we wonder. For what cruel attentions does she still lie down? Our husbands, how they tremble at the very sound of their hearts, not to mention Mother's stuttered welcome: "Come in, come in. This isn't the Ritz, but it's my home."

My sister is sorry Mother couldn't keep this house. "But Mother needs looking after. That much is clear," my sister says.

I agree—the smell of Mother's house! Everywhere, but in the attic, the insistent odor of cat from all those cats Mother kept alive long enough for them to fray the chairs and spray the curtains before meeting bloody deaths. Mother never should have had cats!

Here in the attic, at least, it is fragrant and dry, flamy grains of wood and moted air—still. We are guessing a long time ago Mother did rough cleaning here, and then, as with so many rooms, she shut the door, forgot. Think of what we have found in these closed-off rooms: old chocolates in drawers and sample perfumes and pulverized tablets, a mint-flavored dust fouling the drawers. Tin cabinets, their rusted shelves threatening as old razors and full of medicines—we have cleaned the cabinets of aspirins and strips of pills for allergies or sinus or whatever it was that day. "If one is good, two is better!" Mother was always saying, ready, unready, impatient, slapdash, our Mother, repairing furniture with florist clay, leaving spoons to pit in salt, and books! We find books somehow gone moldy, with only scrub outside: buckskin landscape, thin clouds. Coyotes, wolves, bigger cats—whatever it was that got Mother's kitties is out there in the desert. "You can see from the attic," I tell my sister. Eroded, arid country this is, agave stalks and cholla thickets, creosote in the wash.

"Look!" I say. "The distances—how chalky!"

But my sister says she doesn't want to look. She wants to be home now and not here clearing out, calculating, wondering how long Mother means to live. "It seems purely in her power," my sister says, and she talks about the glasses we have found, lipsticked rims and salty residues from whatever it was Mother went on drinking. "I warned her," my sister says.

"I didn't," I say. "I sometimes bought it for her."

"No!" my sister says, and her face is open, all sur-prise. Does she wonder what else I have done for Mother? Does she suspect how many times I have let our Mother smoke, then watched her wave her hands at me for help to breathe?

Bad daughter that I am, I have bought her favorite kind.

I have gone along in the top-down car with Mother driving fast on empty stretches. The trees chink past, chink past a watery green, and the fields that I remem-ber are smooth and yellow. We want to lie down in them, and, *ah*, until we get to trees again, when Mother presses forward, reckless to get there: home or away from home. "May this never happen to you," Mother is saying, when everything has happened to Mother. Stillborns missing necessary parts, men who turn out to be dangerous. Sickness, excess, indulged goutish heart—her kind of dying. I shut my eyes and listen to us coming into houses—such quiet on these streets and the sound of Mother's scarf in its furious beating. Out in the desert, too, there is the sound of Mother's scarf, its harsh snaps, its language: *I want, I want, I want.*

"Don't tell me what," my sister says, then tells me what it is she wanted: to see Mother grow the old of old ladies in their skeletal nineties—so papery and thin, their deaths seem just a blowing out and not this messy, limb by limb–seeming, slow dying Mother practices. My sister says, "She won't be around to see my children."

"You don't know that," I say. "She could always come back."

This man-size woman, my mother, I have seen her home from hospitals, pulling herself up by the window of the car, growing taller and taller until she stands full height, taller than all the mothers I have ever seen and wearing her body as she might a loose coat— tissues off the tongue of her turned-out pocket—leaving hair and mouthprints wherever she has been.

My sister says, "I was too young. I missed the early miracles."

I look at Mother's legs, how they stand up by themselves in the attic. Whom will Mother find to kiss her now is what I wonder, thinking of Mother in the cranked-up bed, wearing someone else's old mouth.

"You," I say to my sister. "You're the one who nurses her. You look for the bruises. Helping Mother in and out of tubs—you, you dress her, when I won't even touch her clothes, when most of what I see of Mother puts me to sleep."

Her old-lady feet! The monastic growth, the narrow, curling yellow nail of her big toe, the little thorns of all the others—such feet should be covered, I think, but my sister talks of pedicures. The ticktock of Mother's feet under the sheets, the vacant rooms, the hospitals, do not scare her.

I am not my sister. I will not put salve on Mother's sores or comb the smoky hair that flares off her high forehead. Mother's damp heats repel me.

"You are good to her," I say. "But she is worse when you are around. Then she plays the baby, and you feed her. It makes me sick to watch her pulling on the spoon—and you! The way you scoop food off her chin!"

"What else can I do?" my sister says, smiling at the faces I am making, the querulous mouth and shaky hand, the what, what, what that is me playing Mother, fumbling her way to ask, ''What did you girls do last night?'' And the night before that, and the day, the day before, the winter, the spring, the rebuking summer—all gone by while the nurses have been turning Mother, keeping Mother clean in a clean bed.

The nurses, I half-expect to see them in the attic, in the fumy cedar closet of the attic, nurses, heavy and alike as the clothes bags my sister carries, another and another. Nurses, the ones whose upper arms strain even the sleeves of their coats, I have seen them hoist Mother. From under her arms, they lift her long body. They say, ''If you're going to live on your own, we want to see you out of bed. We want to see if you can vacuum.'' The nurses say, ''So,'' giving her a dust cloth and a can of cleanser, leaving Mother with her walker in a space that could be hers. ''Are you up to it,'' the nurses ask, ''this independent living?''

''I have no patience,'' I say, and watch the collapse of clothing bags, tilted as for a fire, ready to kindle— if we had the courage.

But nothing much here would burn entire, I think, only slowly in a noxious stink of plastic, canes smoking into lips, braces stumped as closed-off joints on amputees. A fire such as this would be all smoke.

So what are we going to do with these appliances, these sheets? Such things, so evidently used, are they ever used again?

''Would you sleep on these sheets?'' I ask my sister—and these are good heavy sheets we have here, warm, heavy sheets. They smell of bandages and soap.

No, she shakes her head, which means, I guess,

we'll throw them out like so much else toward the making of the new house, the house Mother always said she wanted: "Hose down, no care." And she has almost achieved it there in the hospital with the nurses she calls out to by name. "Nancy, Laurie, Gail, come in and meet my daughters." These smiling nurses with stories of us in their eyes, we have met them before. "Yes, yes," the nurses say, pinching off the dead heads of donated flowers, standard arrangement—no smell. But there is baby's breath and a foil balloon that some-one has tied to the rail of Mother's bed. This could be a party, a birthday party, but this is every day where Mother lives: dessert as something special, as having come from someplace special, sheet-cake occasions down the hall or weddings bonged across the street. "What a treat!" the nurses coax. "Sit up, dear. Eat," they say, and I see, or imagine I see, the soldier that is Mother, the yellow opalescent skin on her thin arms, her thin arms trembling to raise herself from bed. Oh, why should it be strange how, loving death the way she has, our mother wants to live?

Outside the attic window, there are no streets, only scrub and scratchy plants, wind or quiet, dust—dust enough for me to write Please Wash Me on the window.

My sister holds a broom and sweeps.

AN UNSEEN HAND
PASSED OVER THEIR
BODIES

My son is coughing in his sleep next to me in my bed, where he has come to spend what is left of this night. My son's cough is red, noisy, and loose, a clattering wagon on its jagged way down, with me all ears to the racheting sound of my child-self in the bed next to Dad, who is tossing and threatening. "Stop coughing," Dad says. "You'll wake the dead." Bat flap and smoke in the dark of his voice make me hold back this need, hold back from Dad, whose fleshy skull clenches every raw cough I cough. I want to be still. I fix on the chafed, pitted folds at his neck with a promise to sleep, as if my quiet could ease and uncoil this turned-away man, but I can't and it's out, rude air through the pipes, a dry sound full of rust. Dad says, "I'm too old for this." He says, "Oblige me," and I watch the words turn in this room he calls his own,

Dad's porch, sleeping headquarters, off-limits. How did I get here, close enough to smell him? That's what I want to know: How did I?

Rolled, damp toweling—the kind Dad sometimes swipes at me—he smells like that. He smells like shaving water, where he floats his brush and lets me blow apart the suds before he snaps a towel, says, "Out. That's enough; go get dressed." I only pretend to leave. He never shuts the door all the way, and I want to see, and I can, if I am careful, if I am clever. From where I am hiding, just outside the bathroom door, I can see him. I can see him oiling his back under the sunlamp. It makes me feel lazy just watching him: the way my father massages himself and rolls his shoulders in this heat. So much heat, so much white in wild refraction off the swivel mirror; I see he has to squint to see the parts of himself in the magnified side, where the black eye, lashless and fast, his eye, finds me.

I am almost sure of this—that my father only pretends I am not there.

Like he pretends in his bed this dopey snooze; says, "I give up"; says, "Let me just shut my eyes."

Am I not the woman he cannot keep out?

I want to wake him still.

I want to shrill in his ear: "Look, you!"

But the thought of him makes me close my eyes, try to sleep, a girl.

I hold to the edge of my bed and watch him sleep. I don't move. I let my son take up all the room he wants, knowing he will slip away before I am even awake, and even after I have been so quiet, so good.

THE ENCHANTMENT

S omeone else was in the room, I think—the second
wife. High-parted hair, lips absently applied—the
second wife had been the one to go on talking to my
grandfather. Not the first—the first left, licking salt
from the wide rim of her glass; the third, we knew,
was spending Daddy's money. My grandfather said
to me, "We wanted you to hear this," and I think I
remember it happening this way; there was another
in the room, not just my father and my grandfather
but my father's second wife.

We were told—my grandfather told us, speaking
to me, "Your father is tired; he needs a rest."

I saw my father's head fall forward—monk's bald
spot, mad curls. Broad, broad-hearted, rufous chest, a
squalling red—my father was alive and in the world
and feeling everything extremely.

Did she move to touch him, the blur behind, whoever else was in the room—because I didn't. In the
face of that face then lifted to me, I smiled to hear him
name a place, which when I heard it, I might even
have been there, or else my memory is so profligate
and willfully confused, but I think I always knew this
place where my father was going. In a long car that
gentled over the grated threshold, my grandfather took
him, and sometimes, me, past swells of lawn and more
lawn, wind and slashes of high blue sky in the heads
of furious trees. Odd men they were I saw standing
in the spiny leaves, pinching winterberries; bent-over
figures in discourse with the air. How could my father
sleep here? I wanted to know, but the second wife was
in the car, too, saying it was hard to be surprised this
way, come upon by family.

"Visitors is what we are. We won't stay long," my
grandfather said, and we had made it through the
lunch when we saw the other slinkers in the damp
strawed beds, heard them call, "Professor!" bow and
smirk; and I thought he seemed pleased, my father,
until he turned to ask, "Why this?"

"Why what?" my grandfather asked. "Tell me
what. What are you asking? What is it you want? Do
you know what you want? Do you know what you
are doing?"

My grandfather said, "You have no idea," but my
father kept behind, speaking rapidly, voice soft, my
father asking why when the windows whirred up, and
he was left turning in the turnaround to see us go. A
man in a short robe, left unsashed, how did it feel to

him, I wondered, the worried, furrowed inside seam of his short robe's pocket?

In the coats he left behind, I had gritted my nails on the inside seams of Father's pockets, gritted and sucked them clean.

I did not see him then for a time that passed in the way of winter, colorless and stubbled and flat. The days clicked past same as hangered linens from my grandfather's laundress, underwear cupped in puffs next to slips—my own, only my own, nothing of my father's the way it had been when we shared in the last house a dresser, a closet, a bathroom down the hall.

My father's knocking, I thought I heard it, and I remembered.

"What," Grandfather said, "you must remember what."

"See here," my grandfather said to the company— not her, but men like my grandfather with vacation faces, smooth and oiled and brown. Same suits, thin cuffs, glint of heavy watches when they signed. Here and here and here—so many papers.

"What am I a party to?" she asked when she arrived, knife-pleated skirt and filmy blouse, spectacles for reading, a pair for seeing out.

"This," my grandfather said, as surely as he cleared his throat or pulled at his eccentric too-big clothing;

and the second wife came to where we stood hooding our eyes from the dazzle at the window. Water from such a height was a dizzying coin—that, and the hard shore, the palings of trees, and closer to the house, at our feet from the window, the raw paving of my grandfather's terrace, a stony estate designed to withstand winters that cracked the very roads—to whom now would all of this be given?

I didn't quite ask, really. I hoped to be polite. "How much do you have, Grandfather? For how long has this been yours?"

My grandfather said for as long as he remembered. He was born in the bedroom where he once slept with a wife. He said, "I have always been comfortable."

I wanted to be comfortable.

In the sunroom with the easy men in pearly colors, I spoke freely of my father and of what I had seen with and without wives, waking to my father in his sleepless disarray, a man in tears, kissing my foot and saying I had saved him—my father always threatening death—rolled playbill in his pocket, at my face his sugared breath: We should, we should.

"Yes," she said. "I have seen him with her in this way and been afraid." His temper, for one, as when the milk had boiled over—scalded; and of course, he wouldn't drink it, but argued through the rising light before he took his sleep. "Insomniacs," she said, "are true accountants; they are smug about the time they keep. But he sold the family silver," she said.

"He is not rich," my grandfather said.

I did not tell them what my father had bought me, but I wore the earrings and the small, slight clothes he had said I would grow into—and I had. Even as my grandfather spoke, I was lifting off elastic from where it pinched me.

Breasts, my own.

Breasts, hands, long, thin feet and water-thinned soles—mine—walking the cold stones of my grandfather's terrace, the cold knocking me just behind the knees every time; but not so with her, the second wife in broken shoes, a generous sweater; she was warm.

She asked, ''Did you ever think I heard you? Did you wonder if I knew?''

I had wondered if there was other breathing in the room, a greater dark near the doorway rimmed in downstairs light, and which wife standing, the second, third, or first—in this way alike, watching or sometimes driving for him when Daddy said he could not concentrate to drive—made sick by just the entrance at Grandfather's gate.

''Was it for money that we came here?'' I asked— all those Sunday dinners with the slavering roast sliced bloody on the tines of the carving tools, Grandfather's rare meat and garden vegetables, not the lunch we had on visits to my father's last new place, but Sunday dinner and the long white afternoon in a room where we sat reading until supper.

Quiet, the gaping stairways still and cold, cold air hissing through the sills—the rooms I looked into were dark and cold except for where my grandfather was reading Sunday's papers after the visit to my father; or it might have been after the visit from the pearly men—or any Sunday, really. It might have been that we were alone, long years alone, my grandfather and

I, the wives fled and the cook's night off, so what were we to do but what we did? We took the afternoon's roast, and it seems to me this happened: My grandfather gave me a knife and fork and said, "Take what you want," and we cut into the bleedy meat and picked at it standing, not bothering with plates, with no one there to scold for what we did, pouring salt into a spoon of juice and drinking from a meat so raw it still said Ouch! at a prick from the tines of my grandfather's enormous bone-handled fork.

My nails were grimed with cinder, my lips a smear of grease.

Complicitous season, winter, the day blacked as sudden as did the hallway from my room to his, and we often did not make a visit to my father. We often stayed at home, saying we would only have to turn around again, and so we did not visit—or phone, as my father complained to me, brushing his lips against the mouthpiece of the phone, voice over ocean on the holidays' connections, sometimes cut off.

The way my father talked! Tremulous show-off, he was, all fustian to-do when in the last new place we saw him with his friends, the same we always caught peeking in on us together. "Still here!" my father said, as if another place were possible. "Come in, please, come in." We were introduced again, but I remember no one's name. Even the faces are gone. We had come to see my father. Grandfather and I— and sometimes the second wife—we hadn't driven this far just to shake some soft hands.

"So why bother?" we agreed, and I often didn't

see my father. Easy to make excuses in the gaudy life—
fourteen, fifteen, sixteen—riding on my way somewhere and smoking a cigar, stinking up the driver's
daddy's car.

"I live here," I said by way of a good night at my
grandfather's door, yet forgetful of the driveway lights,
which shone through falling snow, pooling white on
white when next I saw them.

Morning, my grandfather at the table talked of
lights left on. He said, "You are not with your father.
There are rules in this house, remember," rules I was
told my father never followed—which was why, then.
The inexorable logic, how hard I worked to live by it
as Grandfather's darling. No thank you, no I couldn't,
no, please, to what he took from Daddy to give to me.

Petting my watch on any Sunday's visit, my father
said to me, "So the old man won't die with it still on
his wrist." Lucid on the subject of anyone's belongings,
noticing the second wife's new rings, my father seemed
alert to the getting. The shadow boxes and the canes,
the grandfather clock, the shoehorns, the brushes, the
studs, the links, the pins—such enameled old blue—
my father knew the history to and wanted them. He
said so. My father said to my grandfather, "When were
you last dancing?"

My grandfather's smile had teeth for this part. Such
things as he had were his to give, which he did when
he was not afraid of dying—or so my father said. My
father said to my grandfather, "Maybe not dancing,
but traveling—are you thinking of traveling again?"
To the places I had seen in photographs—Grandfather

backdropped by the walleyed rams at Karnak—would he travel there again, as once he had, a young man in a high collar, unused to such heats, yet smiling?

Upright before whatever scene the camera found him, my grandfather had traveled, had been to, had seen the famous cities before the modern wars rubbled them. He had plundered the shops famous for their porcelains and brought home plate and platter and sconce: the teardrop chandelier above the table where we ate, and the canes, of course, from London. I heard him speak. Those are Portuguese, those Italian, but the bronze Diana—oh, God, who knows from where? "I bought it," he said, "but your grandmother was offended by the figure's upturned breasts. Your grandmother," he said, "you can imagine how she suffered your father's first attack, the second—all those wives."

Grandfather's disappointment, I could hear it in his voice when he said his good nights, the way the words came out words—and was it with some longing, and for what, from a man who had had and had? Mistresses, my father told me, he had glimpsed in the crowds of the company parties, ladling the punch, stacking plates high with sandwiches. "My poor mother," my father said.

Sometimes on our Sunday visits, my father cried to remember her. "Mother, Mother," he said while my grandfather looked on and the second wife coughed, embarrassed.

The way my father dressed, grown fat from too much sleeping, in mismatched clothes, seedy as a poet now that he knew himself as poor—and happy to be poor. Look how he was loved, and he pointed to the men who swayed at his door, saying, ''Professor James, sir, may we come in, please?''

''Don't ask them in,'' I said. ''Be someone different.''

Be one of the boys at the concerts, at the ceremonies, at the breakfasts. They rarely spoke of my father, or if they did, it was, ''How's Jim?'' How was it at this last new place? Expensive as hell was what my grandfather said, but we wanted him well again—didn't we?

My grandfather said, ''Poor Jim.''

The second wife said, ''Of all the men.'' She said, ''I gave him you, didn't I?''

But everything we did, I thought, we did for money.

In my grandfather's house, I was given the room with the western view that lit up the matchstick winter trees, a book's worth at a strike—wasteful, too early, short. Winter afternoons, pitched in dark, we sometimes slept in the library, lap-robed in Sunday's papers, my grandfather snoring clogged snores from stories. Warty giants who lived in caves beyond the umbered forest—my grandfather was like one of those in his sleep, or that was how I saw him if I was first to wake. I saw the large sore nose, its old-age red, and the rest of him brown-speckled like an egg, and yet I kissed him.

''Too much,'' my grandfather said. ''That's enough.''

There was more he was saying, except I moved

away with my part of the paper, which was never Grandfather's part of the paper. His part of the paper was nothing to read.

My father said he could not read. He said, "Now they've got me on this stuff, I can't concentrate. I can't see. All I do is sleep and sleep."

I had never seen my father asleep, never known him to be other than fever-pitch awake; flame-tip skin and heat I had felt from his fingers at my cheeks. Not afraid of touching, my father was not, and his roiled speech—sometimes hard to follow what he said. "These drugs," he said. "It's not my fault"—any more than he was here in this last new place. "My own father," my father said. "He did this to me."

"Did what?" I asked. Left alone sometimes in his room to talk, we talked about my grandfather: hard as the stony place that he had made into a home—and me in it. What was he doing with me on the estate? was the question.

My father lifted at the skirt of his short robe. He asked, "What does he want from you?"

I scratched him.

"You would think we were lovers," he said, and I hit at his arms, pushed at his chest with the heels of my hands, pushed at the softening parts—at his belly. He laughed and then grew angry and slapped small slaps fast, all over me, until I was backed up against the door and crying; surely, a snotty, messy kind of crying, the body in an ooze, although what I remember is the joy I felt to call my father fucker—"You fucker."

I told my grandfather, "I wish I were yours." Almost any Sunday I said it. Even if the second wife were present, as she sometimes was, I said, ''I never want to live with my father again.'' The second wife thought it best, too. In my grandfather's house, there was routine: cook's soft-boiled egg in the morning and a table-set dinner each night. Not as it had been with Daddy, the second wife was sure of this, how it was with my father—she had known me eating at the sink from a bag, school shoes still missing and late for school—yet she had let my father drive me.

''Good-bye. See you later. See you next Sunday, next month, next year. You wouldn't want me to give up work. None of this, of course, means I don't love you. Remember how it was. You understand. This is better.'' Any one of us could have said as much.

Besides, I wanted every morning to break up buttered toast into the eggcup.

I wanted lots and lots of new clothes.

Keys to the car, plane ticket, passport, backstage passes.

I wanted to be between visits on a Saturday when we walked Grandfather's gardens—him with the pruners in his pocket and a cane he used to beat at things while he pruned in rolled-up sleeves. The steeped-tea color of my grandfather's arms, sure in every gesture, aroused me. I wanted to brush against and lick him: the pouch at his neck, his white, white hair. Stooped, skinny, abrupt in motion, loose clothes slipping off, my grandfather used his pruners. He worked beneath a weak sun and did not sweat or smell of anything more than his ordered soap, green bars with age cracks that looked like saved stones from the bottom of the lake. The lake, from whichever angle we looked, was chipped blues or grays, or buckled, as with ice; and when it was ice, we stayed indoors. We watched for winter birds—blood smears in the trees or the blue jays he detested swinging on the onion sacks and pecking at the suet. The snow was dirty; shucks of seed skirted the trees. There were pawprints and footprints and dog's canary piddle—too many visitors on any one day.

I'm sorry, I get confused.

The snows that filled the wells of ground about my grandfather's gardens were unmarked and falling in the lights I thoughtlessly left on.

My father was sick and had been sick for as far back as my grandfather could remember.

Imagine what it was like to have a son who said such things!

But what my father said about me! I had heard him before on how it was with me—me, a hole, a gap, a breach, a space, an absence and longing. Empty. Feckless. Stupid.

"Who can ever fill you up?" my father asked.

Then I was using something sharp on him, just to draw a little blood. I was being showy and so was he, my father—he knew about acting. He was smiling while I cut him, so that it must have been the second wife who screamed—not me. Why would I have screamed? My grandfather in the room saw what I was doing.

METROPOLIS

The things my son may see living with me—the way the windows darken suddenly in our apartment, the night tipping shut, a lid, such things as have happened with me and men—shame me. Somewhere obscured in the obscuring city is his father, we imagine. My son and I stand at what was my window, my room, where now another man sleeps, if he sleeps. But he is gone, too, in these early, strangely inky evenings—rarely blue when we stand at the window, and my son asks, "Where do you think Dad is now?" I do not know the answer to this or to lots of other questions my son might ask me, which may be why my son is angry.

Teachers, mothers, women mostly, tell me my son is angry. They tell me this in the way women do in stories about other boys now pacified and prosperous in the alchemy of growing up. "But these boys were once angry," they say, prayered hands and lowered heads. The women carry the word *angry* into talk as with pincers. Bad, bad to be a boy and swinging something he is using as a weapon against a wall.

Should I start at the beginning, then, I wonder, when the rage I felt bleeding on and off for weeks made me needle myself to bleed this child out and try again? I wanted a someone committed to staying. But my son held on; I thought he had to be a girl. The boy's head lifted to view in his easy birthing, the doctor said, "I think it's a girl," and that was what we saw, the doctor, the nurses, the father, me. Before the boy part slipped out, we saw this bright girl mouth pouted for kissing. "Ah," we said.

The astonishing heat between my legs after my son was gone I remember, me on a gurney in a screened-off pen and calling out for ice.

"Do you have any thoughts?" the teacher asks me when I go to see her about my son. But the brown-leaf color of the desks, the exhausted chalky air, streaked with light as if by candles, the tallowed apprentice quality of objects, crude child maps of the explorers, all catch in my throat like ash.

The dying man who sleeps in what was once my bed sleeps poorly and smokes, listens to the radio. My thoughts are of him and of what my son may hear when the dying man comes home, sanding the floor with his long and heavy feet. Up and down, up and down, past the locked bedroom where my son and I sleep, the dying man moves. He calls out from what was my room, "I am dying. I am dying in this fucking bedroom." Night after night, I hear him. Pressed against my son in my son's bed, I hear the dying man and wonder, Does my son hear, is he really sleeping, and how is it I have let this happen to us—opening the door to men who come in or who do not come in, threatening ruin, slapping money on my bureau, saying, "I am dying," or "This is all I have," or "This is all you want."

The teacher, I imagine, has no troubles with money or with men dying. Heavy ankles, yes, and plainer, pulled-back face, but no debts rattling behind her; the teacher wears grown-up clothes and knows how to tie a scarf. Plump and silky, it settles at her neck; I would pet it but for my chewed-up thumbs that seem to snag whatever nice things I touch.

"Anyone would leave you," the dying man says.

I want to tell the teacher that the dying man has newsprint on his fingers, and that my son has seen things, too—the staples in my head.

"You're upset," the teacher says. "Maybe you don't want to talk."

I shake my head, saddened and amazed.

At home, my son has seen me mad enough to kick in glass, blood pooling in the cuff of my shoe.

My son's wet mouth, I could drink from it still.

"I don't know what to tell you," I say to this teacher, and want to hold out my hands and feel a ruler on their backs. Bad, bad to be a woman, indiscriminate and needy, linking arms with any man who promises relief.

The teacher, I think, knows this and all else there is to know about my carelessness.

. . .

Here's scary—a man downstairs in a small light, drinking—and a woman just above him, waiting in a dark bed. From last summer this was, or the summer before; we were in a cabin in the country. The kitchen floor was dirt. Combed black dirt, it stuck to the wet around my son's mouth—there was no end to cleaning my son—no end to cleaning the cabin. Hypnotizing dust motes I remember and the pine furniture ablaze in the late-afternoon sun, corn silk and fruit flies, spoons stuck to breakfast dishes.

The dying man has called out for his mother in the middle of the night. I have heard him and have sometimes answered his call, banged my way through the dark to the foot of the bed where he sleeps and asked, "What is it?"

"He is angry," the teacher says, and she describes my son in the class, talking softly as he does, growing louder—the sly smiles to friends, the audacity, the tinny glare about the boy defiant. Bored or hungry, sometimes ignorant of what inspires him to speak, the boy says he does not know why he does it. "A monologue," the teacher says, "with glancing reference to the class; otherwise, just bloodshed."

My son's drawings are all of men.

I see small heads, squared bodies—a robotic, bolted quality about them, no knees, didactic jaws. They are armed; many of them smoke. Trails of ash and fire are the loose horizontals in these drawings of stiff men standing in air, guns pointed and firing. The blood splatter is colored in.

"Is this normal?" I ask the teacher, and she says she does not know, that she only wanted me to see.

Back-to-back on the acrid, skinny mattress we shared in the cabin, we lay apart and still.

I want to tell the teacher I don't sleep with the dying man anymore, but that there is the night to be got through, living around the dying man, leaving something in the kitchen he may or may not eat, then locking ourselves in, my son and I, in my son's room. How quietly he lies when I scratch his arm, me under the covers of the boy's bed, which means I'll stay the night—tonight, the next night, and all the nights I lie in wait of the dying man's dying.

In the early morning, me in the closet, standing in to dress out of sight of where the dying man worries what I owe him—inflationary calculations, sums figured in the sleepless night, the old harangue—I like it. I feel the luck of my good health, and walk past him wearing it, walk around the bed where the dying man lies, leashed and wounded, yapping at me.

Soon, I think, the dying man will be dead, or he will be gone to wherever it is dying men go in a city—to other women, to other apartments, to other parts of the metropolis.

The beginning is always so sweet. They bring good sheets from some life before and a saucepan, saying, "Can you use it?" Great-Someone's dishes and one or two trinkets from the mother-source, which I have sold, lost, broken.

I have done much damage.

"I told whoever called for you that you were dead," the dying man says, home early and sitting on the bed.

I ask, "How are you now?"

He says, "What do you care?"

Everything in the bedroom is purely itself, doorknobs, windows, dishes of loose change—and I am afraid. I am afraid the dying man will always be here, picking at his scabs, sniffing at his farts, wiping at his face with this day's dress shirt, leaving smudge and oil and threaded juices of himself on what surfaces he passes as he goes about his dying.

This is no place for children, I am thinking when I hear my son call out, "I'm home."

TO HAVE AND TO HOLD

I have accidents in the Fifth Avenue kitchen—cuts, falls, scaldings. What could I be thinking of when I scissor through a plugged cord? My sleeve catches fire on the burner, and all I do is watch its crinkling into nothing. Fast as paper, it burns, filling the kitchen with a stink of burnt hair, my hair, and that is what finally makes me run for the salt, the smell of me catching fire.

Worse things happen in the kitchen—my husband tells me he is in love with someone else, and what do I do? I go out and buy he and she gerbils to make us feel more like a family.

I hate the gerbils. Nothing about them is cute; they twitch and gnaw. The animals live in a plastic night-glow cage set next to the stove, because this kitchen is small, even if it is on Fifth Avenue, and here they scrabble and play and shred their tray paper—dirty animals that eat their own tails.

The girl was the first at it. One morning I found her dragging her rump through the shavings, scooting around the cage, past the boy. His tail was whole; hers was stubbed, pink, wet-looking. I saw her giddy chase of it. I thought, Maybe this is a mating ritual; maybe this is natural. What do I know? Except a few days later, some of the boy's tail was missing; now both of these cannibals are nearly tailless.

This eating has nothing to do with making baby gerbils. I don't think the two of them even like each other. When the gerbils escape from their cage—and they escape every night, squiggling through a gnawed-away part—I never find them huddling. I might find the boy under the sink, the girl near the warm and coiled back of the refrigerator. I catch them up with a dishcloth; I can't stand to touch these addled savages—who could?—especially since they've started eating themselves.

I want to know why my husband picked this woman to love, this woman who has been in my kitchen, who once helped me dry the silverware. This woman my husband loves is always, always on my mind here in the kitchen, where she once hugged me good-bye in her fur and pearls. I split open the coals of feeling to feel the buckle on her belt heat up in my hand. I touch her skirt and the stitched spine of her high heels. I am in a kind of hurry. I snatch at her nylons, her bag. Her bag is the color of toffee; I could eat it; I could gnaw off the clip to where the lining riffles with the scent of her perfume and pennies and lipstick. Would she want to trade her clothes for my kitchen? Does she want babies?

The Fifth Avenue kitchen is so bright and clean. My husband says the counters are still gritty with cleanser. He says the food is ashamed to be seen.

I admit it, I am driven. Last thing I do each night is wash my floor. One of the reasons the gerbils are such a problem is that they are so ridiculously dirty.

I should get out of the kitchen.

I should set the gerbils free.

I should let the scrub pads rust and the inky vouchers stain the counters. I should mess up.

My husband says the fridge door reads like advertisement. He says the door is not a bulletin board. He says, ''Why don't you get a date book, act like other people?''

I thought that's what I was doing: acting like other people. So much space glinting off the white dune of Fifth Avenue: I thought, Other people must want this, but not, it seems, the woman my husband wants. She, he says, wants to pitch her umbrella elsewhere.

Where?

I am standing here with the gerbils, who are loose again and scrabbling over my bare feet.

There is broken glass on the floor.

I can't help what happens.

The kitchen is sprung like an army knife, and I am in a hurry.

I have thrown open the window and am moving fast to catch these gerbils with only my hands. First the girl, who is trembling and trying to nip me—I swing her by the leg out the window; she is gone. Then I make for the boy, hiding in a corner.

I think he thinks he is safe; he doesn't move. Lost, pointless, filthy boy.

I toss him underhand—just like rice.

STEPHEN, MICHAEL,
PATRICK, JOHN

S he wanted to touch the sister's back as she saw it
in the light beyond the door where she stood,
breathing through her mouth, a spy on the sister in
the sister's house—yet waited for, welcome.

"You see that yard?" the sister asked. "That's my
garden."

Gray morning yellowed here and here and pinched
with ribbed red leaves. Impossible to believe that they
had slept through to winter again or that this was
April—and snow, she in the bedroom with the sister,
and somewhere around the house the sister's husband,
caulking windows maybe, wrangling locks. Not much
seen, this husband, but she sometimes heard him brush
against the wall, bulked shoulders and the clack of
buttons. The sound reminded her of parts of him, the

husband's black hair shocked off his wide wrist, his hairy fingers fixing things.

The sister said, "I see a doctor now. I'm on a medication."

"What kind?" she asked. "Since when?"

The sister said, "Since it happened," folding blanket squares and sacks that crackled with static, the sister's hands had snagged on the clothes. "And the sparks," the sister said. Even pulled apart, hand-ironing, the sleepwear had stuck to the sister's palm, and the tips of her fingers had felt coarse to the sister.

The sister said, "I raked the little clothes like leaves into giant bags and lugged them to the basement." She said, "I tossed them. I didn't care where they landed."

The sister said, "Want to know how you can help? You can throw out the flowers. Burst tulips are obscene—black and dusted parts exposed. They don't dry shut or turn to paper. They are never quite dead."

She saw the husband in the yard was waving something away.

"Maybe the dog," the sister said. "You'll hear him howling. It's all very gothic. The neighbors are afraid of us. Everyone, I think, is afraid of us."

The sister said, "The food I buy spoils on the drive home, and you've seen what has happened to my doors. The strips of torn-up bedclothes are to warn off the birds. There is nothing we can do about the howling."

The sister's hands were cutting into pillows, when what she had expected—what she always expected—

was to see fleshier hands, the sister's once, flushed on flushed breasts under cover of their bedroom.

She said, ''What can I do to help?''

Tucking in the bed tight, beating the pillows, the sister said, ''Talk,'' and then they didn't.

White sheets and pillows, white lace curtains very white, and the way the room was arranged, she saw, the high bed, the nightstands, the mournful dresser, all was familiar, was their mother's room, early morning. The light was a salt in her eyes, but she kept blinking into it.

Spit-writing names on the wall, she remembered, and spying on their parents. The sister had dared her to look.

''What do you see?'' the sister had asked her.

''Nothing,'' she had said, when what she had seen was Mother heaving on the stairs, carrying her wrong babies low—Stephen, Michael, Patrick, John.

Her sister stood close to the mirror on the door. ''I'm glad you're here,'' the sister said.

She said, ''I hope,'' and stood near enough to watch the way the soft powder caught in the small lines of the sister's skin, the sister powdering, putting on lipstick— pain for a mouth.

She said the husband was lucky to have her, the sister.

''Really,'' the sister said, dressed and on her way downstairs. The sound the sister made was of soft cloth on cloth.

''That?'' from the sister in the kitchen when she asked. ''That's for bread,'' the sister said. ''I never use it.''

The sister said, "Most of our friends are afraid to visit, I think. I wouldn't visit us if I could help it. I didn't think you'd come."

She said, "Please." She said, "I'm sorry I wasn't here," but she couldn't think of how to finish; she took out the plates instead.

The sister said, "No, he already ate," and she leaned against the sink—they both leaned against the sink and looked out at the yard. They couldn't find him, the husband. The sister said, "Maybe he went into town, or maybe he's around the house too close for us to see."

"We're not good company," the sister said. "My husband is depressed. He sits up nights and drinks. I've called out, 'Aren't you cold? Aren't you tired? Do you want anything?' But he doesn't answer, which makes me more afraid."

The sister said, "Oh, why am I telling you this?"

The sister said, "I was the one who found the baby."

She said, "I know. I am sorry," and she touched the sister's shoulder, put her hand there, softly at first, then firmly, finally to feel how feebly constructed, bones light as balsa wood for toys with daylong lives.

SEE IF YOU CAN LIFT ME

I walk around to the other side of the bed we are sharing, and I put my face up close to hers and say, "Ann, please. Please," I say, and her eyes open, and Ann sees me, I think, and she says, "Sorry" in a loud, steady voice, and she knows. She knows she has been talking in her sleep. In the morning, she will ask me, "Did I scare you?"

The dog, sleeping next to Ann, sleeps through it all. Good, loyal dog he is—this dog and all the others, for as long as I have known her. Ann holds the dog so close, I itch just looking at her bare arm slung around. The bareness of it, that is what snags me, and how she wears these slippery nightgowns—must be cold. Her arm, around the dog, looks very cold and white and dry to me. The dryness especially, I notice this, in contrast to the tops of her breasts, where the skin, I think, is damp. No matter what Ann says, anyone would want to touch her here, but Ann tells me no, only the dog keeps her warm.

Ann says, "You do not know my kind of loneliness."

Ann says, "You have a child."

And so I have.

I used to say my skin smelled of girl from so much touching of my own. Ann remembers. Ann says, "That's when I got my pooch," and she takes his head up in her hands—Ann does this, all the time—and chuffs behind his ears.

Or else she says, "Don't get near me. I smell of dog."

I cannot smell a thing. In this bed again, on my back, I am not near enough to anything other than me; Ann is turned away. She is tucked against the dog, dog pressed against her hollows, which is not the right word for Ann there. Ann is full there. Ann can take hold there, and sometimes does, slapping herself in that place, which, when I am pressing on my own bones, I think of as hollows. The word is *hollows*, but what I see is the flatness of girls.

I see cow skulls.

I see hurtful blue sky and desert, cholla in bloom, places I have never been to but sometimes think I would like to live in with Ann: New Mexico, Arizona, parts of California. We talk about living in these places. Ann says she can see us now at a long table, feeding lots of children. We are feeding some women like ourselves, and some men, too. This part makes us smile, Ann and me, talking about all the people we will feed.

"And not only that!" Ann says. "Not only that. You can buy your girl a horse. Think about it," Ann says.

I do.

I lie next to Ann in this bed and think about us in the houses Ann says belong to grown-up friends, houses with rooms unused for days, houses with two and three of everything, blenders and televisions— closets full of coats of every size. I think about Ann with a man in such a house and doing some of the things she has told me she once did with a man, and I have done, too. I think about breasts—his, hers, mine. I think hard on these breasts or else my mother's breasts come into view, long and unmuscled, and sometimes my grandmother's breasts or my grand- mother's shoulders or the way my grandmother hitched up her brassiere to show off her strap marks to me. My grandmother's shoulders are polished nobs of bone and smell of—but I can only see the cream she is using.

Ann's drinking, now this is something I begin to smell. I put my face into the back of her neck and shut my eyes and see it wavering off her arm like the oily heat that rises off the roads we hope to take fast and sober.

Some team we would make.

Ann drinks through much of the night and likes to eat bread for dinner. She picks at the soft center and dangles the crust for the dog. "I wish you would eat something, pooch," she says; or else to me, "Are you sure?" Ann's nails are the off-white of old candles or honey. They are not always clean—from keeping her hand on that dog all day, taking that dog with her everywhere. I understand that she is tired, but I do not eat her food.

Sometimes Ann says, "Let's have cookies for dinner."

She says, "We are too old to be living like girls!" and we laugh because we *are* girls.

We are eating cereal at midnight.

We are sleeping together in the big bed and keeping a space between. We are still as stones, I think, and dumb as only girls are dumb to how most anyone wants it, someone's breathing.

Ann always says, "Stop looking at me" when I am looking at her, and she pinches me, but I go on looking, smiling this big dumb smile.

I am smiling now.

I am thinking of Ann.

I am thinking of all the women I have seen stepping out of water. Mother, grandmother, sisters, cousins, all different, some remembered. Strong white legs and a black sex worn like a shield; I remember the impulse to kneel. I wonder, Is my cousin still red, and how have men treated her? I look at the way Ann sleeps, curled up against the dog. The last man Ann knew left her with sores. "What a dirty trick!" is what Ann says.

My mother again; I see her hoisting up her panty hose. She is saying, "Is that all you girls think about?" She is getting dressed or undressed or standing at the sink. Mother is saying, "It has been so long since, the parts are grown together." And that is how it looks to me, my mother's smeared gray sex, my grandmother's bones.

Sweet Jesus, I am cold.

Just looking at Ann, the sheet only to her waist and the rest of her pressed to the dog, makes me cold. How can she sleep like this? Why not just use the blankets?

It is cold under the sheets is what I tell Ann, but Ann says, ''We are not in college anymore. We are grown-ups. We sleep under.'' Then she asks me—she does this—for a pillowcase—maybe from the last time? But I am sleeping on last time's, so I give her new, and she hardly sleeps on it, she sleeps so close to the dog.

I shut my eyes and listen for sounds of her, but the only sound is of the dog. The dog is the noisy one. I have heard the dog talk right along with Ann, who lies so still now, I must lean to feel her small adjustments, elbowing a pillow, pulling close the dog to warm herself, as Ann says she wants to warm herself against a person, someone, anyone else; then she laughs at herself. She says, ''What an embarrassing story.''

''Yes,'' I say, now lifted on my arms to see if she is sleeping. ''Yes. Please.''

TEACHERS

She told her daughter as she might a lover such things her lover said were best kept secret from a girl. The color of his hair, for instance—a corolla of metallic light—your mouth went to it. "You had to touch," she said.

"Please," from the daughter, cheeks marked with sleeping and with a salted trail of gargle from the sore that was her mouth. "Sweet girl," she said to the daughter, "stay home from school today, and I will do your hair." But the daughter's hair tangled on the teeth of the comb and stood off her head in surprise.

The daughter said, "I should go to school."

The daughter said, "My mouth doesn't hurt."

"No, no, no, no, no," she said.

"But science!" the daughter said. "History!"

The torchy glare of the art room windows—that

was school as she saw it from the street—and besides, today a winter fog was everywhere, a fumy curling, fishy air, mists shifting against the windows, nothing to see any which way, but you must strain for something known, as to the daughter at the windows, to the crooked nightdress at the windows—a girl, a blue-white like the underside of a wrist, neck and shoulders that same white, small shadows for bones. She asked, "Whatever, dear, can you make out?" and she walked to where the daughter was to see for herself shoes and cuffs under taut umbrellas, hasps to heavy cases.

"What you see is every morning," she said. "We should do something different," and she told about the lover on his way by foot to the sooted downtown where all she knew to say of what he did was eat and smoke. He smoked expensive cigarettes from a foppish country. He tamped them in his overwashed hands. His hands, the sight of which always surprised her, were a white—not her color, not the daughter's—but something sickly.

"Come back to bed with me," she said to the daughter. "We can look at magazines together and figure out what we are doing."

"We should get dressed," the daughter said.

"Today?" she asked the closet, the dresses hanging smally—no expectations, the compact bags for evening in a dust. She said she couldn't find the energy to blow. She said, "Come here," and she took hold of the daughter and led her to the bed. She said to the daughter, "Maybe we should see someone together."

The daughter said, "No, I don't need to talk to anyone, Mother, no."

''No breakfast, either,'' the daughter said. ''No lunch.''

The daughter said, ''Shit school,'' and turned her backpack upside down.

The daughter dressed.

The daughter undressed and dressed again, studding the curled lips of her small ears and rolling bracelets over the heart that was her fist.

Sulk, how easy it was to be a girl and sulk, she told the daughter, watching the girl fold and unfold the gold foil from an empty pack of cigarettes, mumbling herself off to other rooms, seeming a little mad, the way the daughter's eyes flashed when she creaked past the girl—a back, a screen of hair, a voice behind the raised-up neck of her sweater, saying, ''Leave me alone,'' the daughter scoring her journal with a dull pen.

''What are you writing?'' she asked.

''Fuck fuck fuck fuck fuck for pages,'' the daughter said, and seemed happy to say it, *fuck*.

In bed again, she put her hand to herself under the covers and called out to the daughter.

''No,'' said the daughter, ''I don't need help.''

The daughter at the door, the journal spread against her breasts, said, ''I should go to school today is what I should do.''

But the mother said, ''Please, for me—stay home. We could talk about what you would like to do for the summer. Maybe I can find a way to afford it.''

She was looking for ways to afford it, ways to buy mornings with a family in another part of the world or mornings where they both might wake close enough to water. Her hand at the throat of the drawer, she was sweeping after money and talking on the phone. "You may think that living here is glamorous. You may think we're really having fun." Brothers and bankers—men she did not know that well, had never known or had forgotten, she called to remind them, "I have a daughter now."

They asked, "The child doesn't have a father? You have to live in that costly town?"

She said to the daughter, "At least here I am charmed. I am living in history." The cobbling hoofbeats of the Horse Guards on parade, the uphill groans of buses and pauses—a sound as of the ocean, brooms against wet bricks and water-loaded leaves falling to the terrace, these sounds, she knew, and the fences and the roses and the beaded brass details, boot scrapes and doorknobs and lion's head knockers, the cakey houses at the end of the crescent—"If I could go on living here with you," she said to the daughter, "then I would be happy."

"Can I see what you did?" the daughter asked, and the mother, at the mirror, showed the seams, which if anyone had thought to look or if anyone had seen her as her daughter had seen her—mouth skinned of its pleats and swollen as from a beating—he would know what she had done, and he would leave her.

"Do I look that much older?" she asked. But she saw that she was not as the daughter, walking lightly across the room, growing every day lighter, and so moving her to speak of it, to say, "You heartbreaker, you, come back here."

"Sit with me; talk with me; tell me what you are

thinking,'' she said. ''You never tell me what you are thinking. Do you love me anymore? Are you listening?''

The daughter, at the end of the bed, holding tails of fanned hair in front of her eyes, insisted, ''I am listening.''

''I hope so,'' she said to the daughter, and she shook her head with what she knew.

''What?'' the daughter demanded of her.

''No, don't,'' the daughter said. ''I know your dirty business.''

She told the daughter how once, traveling with another man, she was, for a day and a night, sick in a dark bedroom, with only a shared sink at the end of a narrow hallway for water. She and the man were both sick. He had the chills and so did she; they were very thirsty. In the night, he crawled along the floor to the shared sink to wet a cloth, which he carried in his mouth for her to suck on. They were unwell in an unfamiliar room and unable to tell anyone what it was they needed and afraid also of doors along the narrow hallway opening onto the sight of him, a sick man crawling with a cloth in his mouth, so that he did not make many trips, and they suffered; they held together for hours and hours, teething the same wetted cloth.

''Such ways to be pleasured,'' she told the daughter. But the daughter said, ''Don't use that word— please. We are not in Arabia.''

Not in the burghers' town, either, she reminded, not with the boys in Dutchy houses, bonnet-topped and solvent. ''We are not touching up the window frames with last year's paint.''

She said to the daughter, "You won't be able to wear those very much longer," and she was slinging hangered clothes onto the bed—scarf-weight dresses in slick, frictive plastic bags. "See if it fits," she was saying. "Here's this, this. You don't wear a uniform on weekends. You could wear the strapless." The old Bermuda cashmere, the Avenue shoes from a schoolgirl's spring vacation—"Take them," she said to the daughter. "Let me see if it fits," and she tucked behind the bags in bed to watch the girl in furtive dressing and undressing, the scissoring shoulder blades in pulling over, pulling off.

"I don't like this," the daughter said. "This isn't me."

"Maybe not," she said, and she was squinting at the small hardness of the girl in a skirt cocked on hipbones—a body concaved and antlered, no belly to speak of when she whispered in the lover's ear what might arouse him, the daughter's hair, for instance, sharp as packing cellophane your fingers raked.

"I am bleeding," the daughter said, "my mouth."

"Get a cloth," she said, "ice—and not on the bed or that skirt—please, be careful."

"I hate not being at school," the daughter said. "I want to know what they are doing."

She told the daughter it was passing time in school and girls were stalling in the hallways, doing what they do to one another when few men are in sight—and those men old or turned away, often given up to drinking—the girls are pressing close enough to see the wild hairs over the eye bone. They are touching, as they do—sometimes cruelly. "I know," she told the daughter. "I have been in school." Hanks of wiggy hair they hold as if the hair were dirtied—'How often do you shampoo?' they ask. 'Let me try on your rings,' they say, when they have never thought to ask before, wouldn't pluck off stray hairs, wouldn't touch the girl in the mispressed blouse rusty and freakish as a mother's saved corsage. 'These closet-smelly clothes,' they are saying, 'who wants them?'

"Stay home with me," she said to the daughter. "Your lips are swollen. Don't get dressed."

Once hours on the floor doing puzzles, and even earlier, she remembered, a baby in the middle of the bed, so needful and small, she had thought she might kill it—this, and the flushed breasts inflamed from suckling. His thirst, too, the oil he used to ease past the stitches when she was milky and wounded and just to put her foot against the floor to rise from bed as lightly as she did amazed her, as the baby amazed her. "You," she said to the daughter. "I was most afraid of open windows," she said, "when all of my fears were of dropping you, of letting the head snap back against the sill or the sink, you slipping from my fingers into water—sometimes boiling water in the deep pot on the stove. You can imagine," she said, "how I felt about outdoors. Days and days we stayed in; it was too hard to go out. I was afraid of your crying in public places."

"Stay home," she said. "You could make your bed," she said. "If you are so ambitious, you could clean out drawers."

"To find the things that you have left for me to find?" the daughter asked. "I'd just as soon the house was dirty. But his smoke,'' the daughter said, opening windows to the roil and drawing out of curtains with a violating sound—a wind. ''Fuck,'' the daughter said, ''I hate this house,'' and the daughter moved through it, a girl loosely made and brushing against corners—reckless, willful, loud, saying, ''Let's open some windows here. Get some air.''

She followed the daughter. She put her hands over the flutter of schoolwork on the dining table and on the daughter's desk and on the sill in the kitchen—English, found! Something she could read, not math or Latin.

''What is this?'' she asked, holding away the pages, reading how it was for the girl with the man who brought home sand in his pockets, how it was for the girl beside the mother in the bed—sometimes moving against the girl, saying, ''You should know what it costs just to live here.'' School and food and medicine was what the daughter heard, until the daughter promised she would not be sick, but she was sick and often absent. ''This assignment is late,'' written at the top of homework.

But understand—there is this mother! The bath towels, old messages, Q-Tips, hair, the strewn ephemera of indoor living, the unguents for raspy skin, the mother's rubbing in and rubbing in, telling such things that made the daughter wonder—and wonder was this natural, the parts of her the mother bent to? Shouldn't a mother take her sorrow to someone else—to a husband, a lover—a man lying on the bed with his ankles crossed, saying, ''Please me.'' What did a daughter, untucked and scuffed, have to do with their pleasure?

"How awful," she said.

"Hell," the daughter said, angry or tired the way it sounded, almost swaggered, from a girl half-dressed in uniform. Saying, "I wrote that for my teacher"—a girl wetting her broken lips at her mother's ear and saying, "This teacher loves me."

BECAUSE I COULD NOT
STOP FOR DEATH

More than any other, you belong here, but what is there to say but what I meant to say and never did?—not quite and perhaps not even here, and yet I write to you and see your same uneven hand, me older now than you when first we met, my teacher, the oddest-looking man—everyone said so. You were—what, in your thirties?—and worked up every day, spitting into the gullies of books and more books. They have made movies out of you, but the heroes have been handsome—hardly you. Impossible list of imperfections: no chin, moist, petulant lips.

Nora Gail Bryant said you touched her breasts in the cattle-stunned heat of a summer when she was learning words—*ambiguous, augment, assess*—to be the first one in her family to get away from where we all got away from, all but you. Come late enough, by choice, to the new school, where nothing was decided and the unstained wood in the rain flared yellow, you stayed, a pioneer, intrepid. Nora Gail said you—

Oh, we couldn't ever quite believe it. A little tepee of a man—white lashes, goggly eyes—how could you?

I always meant to ask.

Besides, you had a wife then, though for years we did not see that faint-colored woman with a paintbrush at her ear; we were looking at you, you in the middle of the horseshoed tables, waving at us papers with messages in red, words extravagant or cruel. We could see the grades you said you forgot as soon as entered there.

Only the student, marked-upon, remembers.

I am at the end of the horseshoed table, nearest to the board and to you and to where it is you turn to write—in your upslant hand—how much has been said. We are writing poems, and even before the day is out, you are calling to me, "Yes!" You headlonging down the hall after me with the news you like it— "Yes!"

In school, such things can happen as change a life.

You failed me for what I failed to write on Ammons's poem, saying, "So what, impromptu . . ." Your expression as you spoke to me was bewildered; you retreating to your Shakespeare: "You reason as a woman—'I think him so because I think him so'"; you, a teacher, after all, leaning against the blackboard, fanny chalked. You yelled, "Defend yourself!" Names, titles—your readiness to speak made me clumsy, and I resented you and everyone else, pointing: Look! Look at what they do in my house. A morning newspaper, odd magazines; only to Mother do the books collect like string; all kinds, she isn't choosy: hardbacks on the high shelves, but paperbacks mostly—bookmarked with her bobby pins or broken and swollen in the places she thinks to leave them.

I read then.

I read a lot. Mostly poets, men poets, not handsome in their photographs but glistening to please—a sweaty, open-collared pose, an appearance almost anxious, a little mad and full of yearning, a little—should I say it?—like you.

" 'So country-alone, and oh so very friendly,' " you quoted someone, forever old and unloved. "Of course, love," you said when I was no longer your student. "What else but love and God and dying?" you asked. By then only drinking coffee, you sometimes trembled just to speak, and yet I made our dates in bars and pulled olives off toothpicks with my teeth. Conspicuously buckled—links, chains—I tunneled my hand through the gap in my shirt. You told me what you wanted. But I, who had given in to so many with no regard to after, guarded my sweet sex.

We met in places far enough away from where you taught, kept a wife, slushed through the streets after rice, milk, salt; besides, that life—shelves of soups and chipped plates and umbrellas crimping in the closet heat—was not real, no more than were the children, yours and mine. "Boy or girl?" you had to ask—and ask.

But so did I.

"Rousingly disillusioning" was how you said it had been for a lot of us, and you sent me your poems where the vaulted classroom flickered warm-wood red. Your sentiment surprised me; besides, it was not like that. The ceiling was low and perforated—I remember—and the classroom's plastic surfaces, slouchy modern seats and rounded edges, table legs like cue sticks, hollow tubes of aluminum; I could lock my legs around them, writing furiously on whichever Conrad it was in the years I had you. You were interested in islands, you said; the sea, your mother. I sat through our dates, thinking of that classroom and of us here in the middle of the country, no ocean in sight. Dry-level treeless expanse, the same we looked out on and out on from wherever you were staying then, getting well, you said, getting better than ever. Coffee, coffee, coffee. You were warming your hands on the mitt of your cup, sniffing at the vapors, palely seen. You, sick this way, I could and could not believe it. "Really?" I said to every disclosure. "I'm amazed. I didn't know. . . ." Didn't want to know. Your hands were very pale. Your fingernails were yellow. It was easy to resist you, to say no to you when you asked if you might.

I did not treat you well.

I never told you . . . turned away in the moment when it happened, you shutting your mouth on the tablet of her words—Dickinson, the flood subject, Death.

Was he expected?

Were you in any way prepared?

The students gathered at your desk said you were teaching or had finished teaching the famous poem when it happened. But I am not acquainted with these students and cannot ask what it was they heard, children still. Yet every year I greet them, as you did on your Great Lawn, versions of the same faces.

I begin to know how old you were. Death, death apparent everywhere—and you dying too soon for us to talk about it.

HIS CHORUS

The girls had their own versions, of course, which they told, calling her by his name for her, Margaret, saying, "Margaret, we knew your brother. He wasn't bad." Then what? she wondered, and Margaret came upon them again as she had come upon them. Long days, taking the washed streets home from work, Margaret had come upon them, the girls and her brother, bunched under the portico of the night-abandoned embassy, all shiny blacks and chains before a match, another match illumined their sprung faces—surprise!—or else they did not see her, and they argued. Margaret had heard their girl voices in the muffle of the huddle, asking, "Share, will you, please? I'm cold." In the unhinged season this had been, already dark, when the wind off the river rolled barrels down the promenade and banged the padlocked gates of shut-up shops. "Coming home?" Margaret had asked him, and her brother had answered, rolling his shoulders to say, "I don't want it—fuck off, you mother!"

The brother was a shrug, a glance, a long, stooped back, rough hair belted in notched garbage ties—and gone before he was gone: This was Margaret's version. She told anyone at all about the resinous stains on his fingers, the slept-in folds of his shirts. The jeans he wore so long unwashed were oily with his dirt. No coat, no socks, shoes curled witchy and split at the seams, her brother at the lip of things—the door, the curb, the dock—was licking at the fogged face of his kiddie-face watch.

Do you know what time it is? If she could only ask her brother again—do you have any idea what time it is? Margaret folded laundry, pinching at her collar bath towels still warm yet coarse against her chin. What else was there to do? she asked. Margaret told the girls, "I waited up for him at night. I washed the floors." From upstairs came Martin's calling, "Margaret, look at the time!"

Four, five, six in the morning when the sky pearled and others, early wakeful, moved, she guessed as she did, to hoard the spangled outlook, Margaret did not care by then that her brother's bed was empty. "Not one of you girls in it," she said, "and I bet you thought I didn't know, but he told me."

On the nights he did come home, he spoke of the girls. Crouched in the collapse of his bed, he gave his version of the girls to Margaret. How their hands brushed over the new hair under his arms—as though it were high grass and they walking through the field of him. ''My brother,'' she said, ''he told me what happened some nights after you abandoned the abandoned embassy.'' The sucked-down candies he proffered on his tongue. The brother was talking and Martin was calling ''Margaret!''—when who was this Margaret? She sometimes forgot herself with the boy—the boy huffing on his watch and scolding, ''Fuck Martin! Margaret, it's me who needs you.''

She told the girls, ''I had no babies of my own.''

And another time, when they would speak to her of him, she asked the girls, ''He did tell you about us, didn't he?''

''Yes, yes, yes, yes, yes,'' the girls said, which made her wonder then what her brother might have said about her.

He might have said Margaret was his mother, even when their own was alive and making a living at night. He might have described a sister of stout and rounded back, despite that she was young; she was working. She was working dirty jobs in dirty clothes—for him. For him she was broiling cheap cuts done for dinner. For him she bargained; for him she wrote: ''Please excuse this lateness. He wasn't feeling very well. He didn't mean it. He didn't know. He didn't understand.''

The ways she thought to love him! Draping towels over his bent head at the mouth of the steaming pot—to help him breathe when he was croupy— such was her mothering. Margaret was the person he thought first to see when they picked him up for thieving. She never made him promise to quit his ways, but listened to him promise he would try to be better—especially around Martin—no more stripping through the kitchen, drying himself with his shirt. He would not cough when Martin was talking or in the man's presence snipe at her for money. The rinds and open cartons behind the milk—sometimes even a plate, fork and knife crossed over it—empty dispensers and unexpected bills, late-night lockouts and bust-up girls: There would be, the boy promised her, no more surprises.

Was that how he thought to tell the girls it was among them—a sister, a brother, a brother-in-law—in a strip of rooms made smaller if the brother had company?

Because, she told the girls, she was not so old as to forget some sensations; she recognized the knock of the bed and the yeasty smell of yearning. Her brother's broken, coaxing voice—she knew the sound of that: his *please* and *won't* and *will you*. The sore places near his lips and his lips, so split and glossy, were some of what it was about him—must have been—that made the girls say yes, grind their heels against his back, ask, "Doesn't this hurt, what I am doing?"

"No, no, no, no, no," the girls insisted. "We were not like that," and they didn't call her by her married name, but spoke familiarly. "Margaret," they said, and they described her brother as sullen. They had seen him elbow clingy girls, seen him shawled against the chills, seen him counting his money. The way he left the bathroom with his beery piss unflushed in the unseated bowl, the girls laughed to tell it, although Margaret had seen it, too. Suddenly, the brother was leaving his mark in the rooms through which he passed.

"No," she said. "He wasn't such a beast as that." He spent time uptown on the high grounds of the garden with the scrolly gates. "He could be sweet," Margaret told the girls. "He was not indifferent to his surroundings." He looked at trees, at how in spring the new leaves were so many of them spiked. He had his places—that much she said she knew. He sometimes went for drugs. "But, Lord," she said, and looked hard at the girls, "we all of us sometimes need it."

The grassy smell of him come home on an evening when the sky stayed white, Margaret remembered him with blades of grass pressed against his back and with muddy, open shoes. He brought home a smell of something she had forgotten, with Martin in the broad bed crying out, "Margaret!"

Of course, there were resentments, she explained, Martin's version of things, what he called "assaults by that punk-mouthed brother of yours," then added, "Yours the family with the fucked-up genes—lucky you can't pass them along."

"My fault," Margaret said to the girls, hands cupped between her legs. "My fault he was my brother. I could not scold him. I liked to kiss him instead. I liked to rub my thumb along his front teeth, sit in his room and watch him sleep." In sleep, his body was newly heavy and unmarked—breath fluttering the hollow of his neck. She said, "I was meant to see him, but not like that."

"No, no, no, no, no," Margaret cried, but when the girls appeared confused, she said, "Remember who saw him last."

Late night or early morning, the hallway narrowed

to a tunnel in the light from the end where he stood. He was returned but about to leave. His loose clothes undone confused her, but his sideways moves she understood. She had experienced before the unexpected charge of his unexpected smile, the hands lifted as in blessing: good-bye, good-bye!

But wait!

She had been waiting for him; she was awake, brushing aside other versions of his story—the one with the coroner's instruments or the one where the heart gave out softly, and she pointed to that place on herself.

''My brother's heart,'' she told the girls. ''I have heard its tricked beat. I have kept him company here,'' Margaret said, and she opened the door for the girls to see his bedroom, the sheeted windows and the cutouts, things tossed, tented or on a tilt—in some ways just a boy's room, no matter what was written on the wall. Impossible to make out anyway, his aggressive urban scrawl, his tag—whatever was his name—he wrote it where she walked from work past the diplomatic row, the promenade, the padlocked buildings. His bullying design was everywhere she looked.

His face, too, his wounded face—the bruised hollows of his eyes and his eyes so thickly lashed and sleepy—was the first version of his face Margaret saw. Here the skin's imperfections, summer-oiled and overwrought, were more pronounced than in the colder seasons when confronted with the smallness of his face behind a scarf. Outside, or on the way outside, the brother's skin was close in winter, blown clear, cheeks a wind-scratched rouge. Yet she did not move to touch that face or the others that occurred to her out of order but up-to-date. Margaret told the girls, ''Of the little boy he was, I remember less and less.''

A swatch of baby hair—shades lighter—and the slatted cage that was his chest, veiny threading everywhere.

Nails soft enough to bite off.

A new body very clean.

Shoes.

Hands again.

The sweated valleys between his fingers, his fingers ringed at the knuckles—and then not—but squaring at the ends to an older boy's hands, drumming the kitchen counter.

''Hush with that noise! You'll wake Martin,'' she scolded, then asked, ''What is it you want?''

The brother grinned his hungry face, the one he wore when the drugs wore off, and he propped himself against the cupboards. This face was a face she knew regardless of season—slack or sly, it was hard to tell—but his eyelids twitched and his speech slurred in its wavering volume of request. ''Do you still—'' he began.

''Still what?'' she asked. ''What?'' She could not understand! ''What is it you want?'' she asked this brother again and again. ''What is it?''

When anything, she told the girls, she would have given him anything—and he knew this.

He was spoiled.

''Yes, yes, yes, yes, yes,'' the girls said. They said, ''Margaret, we've been there.''

''But he didn't answer,'' Margaret said. ''That time

he was in my arms—flat out on the floor I found him and pulled him up against my knees—his mouth stayed shut.''

''This was in the living room,'' Margaret said.

''I have his watch. I took it off. I thought, What the fuck does it matter to you? Look at all this stuff of his I've got,'' and she started opening his drawers— beer caps, rubbers, cans of spray paint. ''Can you imagine,'' she told the girls, ''the bony rattle of the cans at night and Martin hollering for him to quit!''

''You must have known this about my brother,'' she said, ''surely,'' and she threw away a plastic bag, burnt matches, some kind of stuck-on candy.

''Yes,'' the girls said. ''Yes and no.''

''We knew him first from the yearbook. We guessed his long smile was to cover up his teeth. We thought we would like him, and we did.''

''He found us names,'' the girls told her—okay-sounding gang names from unflattering sources, from defects like moles or stutters.

''Spider was mine,'' a dark girl said. ''Can you guess from where he got it?''

But he was affectionate, the girls told her. He seemed hardest on himself—wedging his narrow body in any narrow space. He said he wasn't smart.

''You are!'' the girls had told him. ''You only have to learn how to work!''

Margaret said, ''I remember his crying. He woke me with his crying—how many times?''

''Yes,'' they said, yes to what she tossed before them: the pink and yellow bodies of the skin magazines, sticky tubes of jelly. "He only told us he was sad," the girls said.

"What for?" Margaret asked. "What was ever denied him?" Margaret said, looking past the girls to see if she could see his knotted chest and arms and shoulders in his furious abandon—shoving, shoving himself against a loose shape whose head knocked against the headboard of the bed. The noise! The noise! The old masturbator from next door, crying out, he couldn't stand it, Margaret; he couldn't stand this fucking boy!

He was a boy.

He woke with his hands between his legs.

He cried out, "Is there anything to eat?" Doors slammed, or else he slunk past in his tired clothes. The light was afternoon light or later—and cool. All day he slept; skin flakes flew up when his sheets were tossed, also fingernails, hair—his hair was anywhere, as was the glass imprinted with his ghostly mouth.

"All this talk about this boy," she said to the girls, when he was just a boy, who lived, a brother with his sister and his sister's husband—in odd arrangement—but who did not these days?

GIOVANNI AND
GIOVANNA

Oh, that these fervent thoughts we have of our dead would sift into their spirit world and warm them with the truth of how they matter to us still, how they are missed. Dale I remember, shy man, large, embarrassed nose and ears, how I often knocked against him, waiting for a ride to wherever it was I was going then, a child, sleeping over, the sheets always cold and a terrible thirst. The dry part of going away, my mouth open to it in the back of Dale's truck, faced forward: all that green air, until I was so dry and beaten—lashed by my own hair—I was exhausted and sad, sad to leave him. I said, "I want to stay with you." I said this to him, sometimes lying. I thought, as children do, that I was necessary, that Dale's life without me was just a run-down house and a wife named Ida.

The pink of Ida's candy pink gums and tail-fin glasses—Ida was ugly in ways even a young girl would notice—me five, six, seven when I stayed with Ida and Dale those times my mother couldn't find her mother to do it. My glamorous mother, of course I would notice: Mother all high color and Ida, muddy hair and eyes—those preposterous pink gums. The way Ida sucked on her teeth after supper—after any meal—but Dale never seemed to mind. Dale, in his damp bib overalls and lace-up shoes, was happy to chew on a toothpick.

The homely everyday about their lives!

They are both dead now.

I listen to your workmanlike exhausted sleep, the gagged intake and hissed release of breath, heel scratch, then the wounded sound in your descent before you startle. Are you awake?

"Are you awake?" I ask.

Nothing.

"Are you?" I ask again, and lean closer to your ear, to you asleep.

How can you sleep in this cheap motel—generic, unmarked, grouted vanity, unmarked surfaces, cast-ered bed?

I saw the foot of Dale's bed in passing, and it looked hard to me and plain—plain as Ida shucking down the hall in pink chenille and mukluk slippers.

Dale's house is the house we see at either end of town, small and white and near the road, muddy yard and broken hedge, a dead car overgrown, and something that may or may not be a fence, a flag and maybe flowerpots from cut-up painted tires—a grill, a laundry line, a dog chained even in the rain. I can hear him still, Dale's Lucky, the shunt and clank of him leashed and whining, rubbing fecal streaks against the side of the garage because the mutt can't reach the house, although the house smells of him—of wet dog.

Onion, there is the smell of that, too, the front door clacking onto Ida's kitchen—the impact of the kitchen—hard floor and mean light, the smell of wet dog. On the steps to the kitchen, big unbuckled boots, openmouthed and panting—I think the boots were animals only waiting to be fed.

Early risers on the road, you buy us soft glazed doughnuts and doughnut-shop coffee, and we eat and drink, driving into the red eye of another yellow morning. You say, "Before we know it," and then attach to this clause whatever is passing—the towns, the states, this summer, our lives.

"Oh, please don't say it," I say.

The corn silk is black-yellow, and there are unexpected, early turnings—bloody leaves and blown weed, bowed fields, picked barrens.

Dale was used to seeing blood, working out-of-doors and with his hands the way he did, and yet the sight of Ida's bloodspurt from the doctor-lanced boil took Dale's breath away. "He fainted," Ida said, right there in the office before them both, Ida and the doctor, looking over Dale—amazed at what could fell a man.

Love—not of the kissing sort; I never even saw

them touch—but shadowing one another the way they did in sickness, toward the end, when Dale's heart had become the thing we knew would kill him —in their every movement bent to each other, love it was.

The special diet, the new hours, the slow, deliberate life Dale slunked in as in a too-big coat, playing at being old and near to dying, when he was not so old, only that he looked it and was afraid.

The mean life I thought Dale led—even so, he loved it and was afraid. He was afraid of being ambushed, so that the clothes he wore were the clothes I guessed he wanted to be found in—ready for it, the next, last bed.

Every day the suit then, brown or gray, the polished shoes, the dark, sour socks. Water-combed his hair and shaved, close-shaved, three times a day shaved and hands washed until the short nails wore away, translucent and smooth as water-beaten glass and not as I remembered—not yours, yellow, bark-thick, carelessly much used and bruised in what you do.

Gardener, laborer, lover—you, I love your thumb, the thumbnail's scrape of me.

In the story of our lives, nothing much happens but that we drive past the same town sometimes and remember. A long time ago and for a long time, I knew them, Dale and Ida. I leave a lot out when I tell you they were poor and childless, so that I thought as a child I was the saving of them—or could be.

They are both dead now even as you drive past the like houses, the churchyards, the graves.

You say, "Maybe we should find a house."

But we like this way, I know, turning in each morning the last room's heavy key and wishing perfect strangers a good day.

Christine Schutt lives and teaches in New York City.

A   NOTE   ON   THE   TYPE

This book is set in a typeface called Méridien, a
classic roman designed by Adrian Frutiger for
the French type foundry Deberny et Peignot in
1957. Adrian Frutiger was born in Interlaken,
Switzerland, in 1928 and studied type design there
and at the Kunstgewerbeschule in Zurich. In
1953 he moved to Paris, where he joined Deberny
et Peignot as a member of the design staff.
Méridien, as well as his other typeface of world
reknown, Univers, was created for the Lumltype
photo-set machine.

Composed by Crane Typesetting Service, Inc.,
Charlotte Harbor, Florida

Printed and bound by The Haddon Craftsmen,
Scranton, Pennsylvania

Designed by Iris Weinstein